For David,

Thank you
For your support!
I hope you
enjoy!

[signature]

THE GARBAGE MEN

by TRAVIS SMITH

The Garbage Men

©2011 Travis Smith

ISBN: 978-1-936447-30-5

This is a work of fiction. Names, characters, places, and incidents either are the product of the author's imagination or are used fictitiously, and any resemblance to actual persons, living or dead, is coincidental.

Designed and Printed by
Maine Authors Publishing
558 Main Street, Rockland, Maine 04841
www.maineauthorspublishing.com

ACKNOWLEDGEMENTS

I would like to thank everyone who has made the completion and publication of this novel possible over the many years of its production, in no particular order:

Bonnie Smith for instilling my passion for literature

Debra and Nathan Hayes for their endless support and contribution

Jeff and Anne Smith for their support and motivation

Mel and Peg Dainty for their generous contributions

Mallory Langkau for helping design the artwork

C. Scott Fleming and Josh Ball for their support and feedback in the earliest stages

All other innumerable friends and family who read and encouraged my manuscript

The staff of Maine Authors Publishing for helping make my dream a reality

And finally, all buyers of this book for supporting the continuation of my career

I thank all readers for helping me actualize my dreams. I hope you enjoy my stories.

PROLOGUE

A small brown bird had been up and about since well before the sun first appeared in the sky. She flew around busily from tree to tree all day, collecting small twigs and pieces of bark with which to line her worn nest. Her eggs had come late this year, and it was prudent to provide her newborn chicks with a bit of extra insulation for the coming autumn.

After working all day, flying from the nest to trees farther and farther away each trip, she stood on the ground beneath the last tree to be searched this day. She watched placidly as the strange machine rolled down the street and collected large bags of refuse. This momentary lapse in concentration left her vulnerable and oblivious to a much larger black bird swooping down from the branches above.

The black bird cawed loudly as it slammed into her full-force, pinning her painfully onto the ground. The moment its sharp claws retracted from her back, the mother bird scrambled frantically forward, hastily escaping the black bird's grip. She alternated between running and flying spasmodically over several yards and driveways in the neighborhood until she was clipped by a moving truck turning into one of the driveways. She landed on the hard concrete on her back and watched a very large man and somewhat smaller woman descend from the truck.

Her heart was pounding in her chest as she waited for the giant man to stomp her into the pavement, crushing and splintering her tiny bones beneath his boot. The skinny woman would surely sweep her paralyzed body away with disgust if the giant didn't kill her first.

Then she saw the smaller human exit the truck. Surely a tasteless, malevolent child who would hold her and break her wings and pluck her every feather before putting her dying body into a slingshot to launch over the trees . . .

Her shock subsided, and her paralysis broke; she took off, flying frantically back toward her own tree, curving back and forth impossibly between the branches. Just when her nest was in sight, her panic-stricken brain drove her to dive beneath a large root that some sort of four-legged creature had dug out of the ground.

But, alas, her frenzied flight had finished, and her right wing became lodged and broken at an awkward angle beneath the large root. She struggled at first, tiny heart pounding impossibly fast, but then the shock set in again, and she began to still. Unwittingly her own worst enemy, the bird's vision faded to black as she saw the garbage truck drive past her very own tree, just meters away.

1

David Slate sat on his desk chair beside his bedroom window watching birds down on the lawn pecking at the grass and each other. He wondered how any creature could be so stupid, so completely oblivious to all around it, at least until it heard something. The slightest sound or movement would surely set them off like paranoid schizophrenics.

Always on their guard, yet completely brainless. How can anything so ignorant have enough sense to get away from something as simple as a human when it needs to? He sighed at the boring notion, though it was strikingly accurate; when a bird hears a noise or merely sees movement from the corner of its eye, it almost surely needs to get away. It seems that everyone is out to get them.

They spend their short lives milling around constantly, using energy only to flee and reproduce. What a petty existence.

Humans are a lot like birds.

It was Wednesday, the afternoon after his first day at his new school. His family had just moved to a suburban neighborhood in northern Alabama. The town was in Thriftson County.

David found that Alabama wasn't completely overrun with hicks as typical stereotype suggests. Sure, it had a few, but what state didn't? Of course it had more than he was accustomed to; he had moved from a crummy neighborhood in southern Michigan. Everyone here seemed to have an accent, too. He had concluded unyieldingly and rapidly that Alabamians' accents sounded nothing short of ignorant and brash. The South easily has the worst reputation in the way of linguistics, and it took David less than half a day at his new school to understand why. He was disdainful of country bumpkins and classic "rednecks," but for no real reason that he could discern; probably just because he had a past grudge against one in particular and held them all accountable for it.

Pop-psychology.

David was an A- and B-student, but how or why his miserable parents kept him in school was a mystery to him. He was very bright, he was very independent—given his family situation, he had to be—and he liked to read in his spare time. Reading was essentially his only real hobby, his only indulgence, so he did it a lot now that he was in a new town with no friends.

That is not to say that he ever had many friends anyway, but here he had none. He was kind and easy to get along with, but people never paid him enough attention, probably because he was so shy and quiet. People were too caught up in their own song-and-dance to bother with something different, something new. Unless, of course, that new thing provided an outlet for aggression and belligerence.

He had endured his share of bullies in his old school (more bullies than friends), and, from innumerable uncomfortable confrontations, he had learned to merely stay quiet and look away, try to ignore the rabble-rouser. He'd never had the nerve or energy to fight back; he found it pointless, in fact. Why lash out at someone who could never be able to understand what you were saying anyway? Anger never showed on his face or in his voice, but it was there, inside: anger and pain unable to penetrate the surface of his contemplative nature. He didn't have an active life, and he rarely cried, so he vented his discomfort with reading; escaping to new, exciting worlds, with their spectacular scenery and their grandiose heroes, was just the therapy David needed.

He'd had about as many girlfriends as he'd had friends in his life: just a few petty girls who had passed him notes in grade two or three. He was bright enough to realize that this was nothing more than a formality among the younger kids, but he, like every other adolescent adventurer, had played along simply because he didn't know how else to respond. Everyone needs to feel wanted; everyone wants to feel needed.

David had an average height, medium-length brown hair, green eyes, and glasses—not nerdy glasses, just average glasses. He was just an average kid of fifteen years, another face in the hall who liked to read and watch things out of his upstairs window. Just an all-around unremarkable kid with little to lose and less to say.

Birds . . . David thought, drowsing *. . . so stupid . . . But they live in complete harmony with their own . . . hopping around mingling all day with other birds, picking at the grass, never pushing around smaller birds,* *or picking on birds a little different from themselves . . .* His eyes closed, and his thoughts began to mix, mild reflection turning to the all-too-familiar self-loathing pity . . . *What did I ever do to anyone? Why am I cast out? When—*

"Davie!" cried a sarcastically sweet voice from downstairs. "Come here, please."

He snapped up with a start. If he didn't know her, he would have thought that she was capable of being in a good mood.

"Aw, man," he sighed to himself. "I was perfectly content sitting here watching the birds and falling asleep . . . I'm coming!"

Janet Slate, his mother, was, in essence, an extremely sadistic woman. He knew that she found so much pleasure in causing him pain. His father, Pete, was a balding man who was so ridiculously addicted to drugs and alcohol that it was almost a problem just letting him out of the house, but Pete, being the sloth he was known as, never complained about being cooped-up. He was also abusive while under the influence, even more so than when sober, so David generally avoided any contact with either parent. He hoped that his father was in his own room so he could evade any confrontations now.

When he reached the bottom of the stairs and turned the corner into the well-lit dining room, he saw that there was no such luck. His parents were sitting at the dining room table with an elderly couple that looked to David like something from *Leave It to Beaver*. Although Pete was in an uncomfortable daze staring at the floor next to the table, he looked a little more sober than usual. The couple was unrealistically dressed in a typical old-man cardigan and old-lady blouse. The woman even had a brass robin pinned to her breast! The most nonchalantly text-book, clean-cut couple David had ever laid eyes upon, they seemed to be from some clichéd movie, as though they carried good neighborly advice or ominous warnings about an inevitable cataclysmic event that would take place at the coming of the next full moon.

"These are our new neighbors," his mother said, cocking her head and seeming to dare David to defy her obvious facade, "Mr. and Mrs. Stewart."

She directed her next statement to the elderly couple. "This is our son, David." Then she whispered to them, but David heard every word. He knew she wanted him to. "You'll have to excuse him. He's a troubled child." Then she added with a theatrically morose cock of the head, "His psychiatrist told us that he may never grow out of it." Leave it to Janet to find a sickening misjudgment in almost everything. While she acknowledged that David had problems, she knew nothing of his troubles, and she would never be capable of acknowledging their actual foundation, which nothing short of her own behavior had constructed. She seemed oblivious to her own obvious social incompetence and was struggling to pass any blame for the awkward encounters on to David.

And it wasn't even true! Even if David needed a psychiatrist, his parents wouldn't notice, and they surely would spend neither their time nor their scant money on trying to improve anything in his life. They couldn't even maintain their own mental well-being. They were cat-sack crazy, and everyone knew it.

Mr. Stewart's eyes darted knowingly and apologetically to David, then back to Mrs. Slate. He caught on quickly. David felt an unfamiliar pang of gratitude.

"Okay, dear, I just wanted to introduce you to them. You may go back to your room." David had never heard his mother speak in such good humor; he had previously thought it impossible. Her pathetic display shined through, David was sure, not just to him, but to everyone in the room.

"I'm thirsty. I think I'll get something to drink first." David said.

Janet's eyes narrowed at David, but he paid no attention and walked past them into the kitchen, knowing immediately that he shouldn't have antagonized them.

"Excuse us," Janet said exasperatedly, "we need to have a word with our son." She gave a hideously fake smile, grabbed her husband's arm, and pulled him into the kitchen after David.

"Look," she said quietly to David, "You will not embarrass us in front of company. Get back to your room now." She pointed a finger accusingly at David as though he were nine years old.

"I don't need to embarrass you. You're doing that just fine by yourself." David said, concealing his own shock at this quick retort, and walked back into the dining room leaving his mother and father dumbfounded.

David exited the kitchen with a steadily pounding heart. He had never stood up to them like that before, definitely never had made any wisecracks, and, despite fear of inevitable repercussions, he felt exhilarated. He normally stood looking in the other direction and saying nothing when his parents gave him grief. This was a very new feeling, a feeling of semi-triumph, but he knew that the victorious notions would vanish as soon as the novelty of his behavior wore off, once the Stewarts had gone back home and they actually realized what he had done. Then they would resume their normal routine, in which they didn't need to pretend to be kind to him for the sake of their own feeble social images, and his father would surely let him know how they felt. He yearned to go to his room, climb out his window, and escape with the birds.

2

As David walked uncomfortably back into the dining room, he remembered a time years ago in his old house: he had been sitting in his room looking out his window at nothing in particular. He saw his mother get into the car and start off to some destination unknown and unfathomable to himself. She stopped at the garbage can and put a bag inside, then drove off on her way. David just sat watching leaves rustle in the wind and occasionally fall from their tree. A few minutes later, a different car pulled into the driveway. He had never seen the car before, but he took no time to see who got out. He got up and went over to his door and out into the hall. Positive that his father was probably stoned and sleeping, David got to the end of the hall and heard a knock. When he reached the door, he saw that a young, attractive woman was standing outside. She had an extremely cheerful face with a smile so wide that David thought her lips might rip at any second. Despite the smile he noticed that she was fidgeting nervously and making an obvious attempt to refrain from biting her lower lip. She looked around restlessly until he opened the door and stood politely waiting for her request.

"Pete?" she asked politely but with a quizzical expression.

"I'm sorry, he may be . . . " he paused, thinking, "unavailable now. I'm David, his son."

Suddenly her whole face seemed to droop. Her smile left instantly, and her eyes, ears, and forehead dropped. She no longer looked young, attractive, or nervous. She wore a mean, disapproving scowl, just like his mother always did when she saw him, as if it were his fault for existing.

"His son?" she demanded impatiently. "Pete's never mentioned anything of the sort." She pushed him away and entered the house, calling for his father.

"Um—" David started, but she had already turned into the living room to find his father.

David stood for a few seconds in silent confusion until, as usual, he decided to ignore the whole situation. Unfazed by such inexplicable occurrences at this point, he went back to his room and sat down on his bed and started reading. Soon, though, he began to hear things from the living room, things he wished he didn't hear, things he hoped he would never hear again. The two shouted at one another at first, just as he had heard Janet and Pete do on innumerable occasions, and then there was a commotion as if things had fallen. When, after a short silence, the sounds became sexual and even more uncomfortable, David turned on the television and turned it up loud enough to drown out the noise, but he couldn't stop thinking about the way she had been biting her lip nervously outside the door.

A while later the sounds subsided, and he heard the kitchen door close, the car door close, and the car ignite, and he looked out the window to see it driving away. He got up to go back to the kitchen for a drink. He passed the living room and saw his father watching the television, as he often did. In the kitchen, David had just begun pouring a glass of water when Pete entered. Though he could hear his father, David didn't look at him (he rarely did); he had his back turned. Pete approached him, grabbed him by the arms, and spun him around fast enough to give him vertigo. "You been peeking in on me?" he demanded.

"Peeking in?" David feigned confusion. "What do you mean? I was reading in my room."

"Don't lie to me, you sneaky little shit. I know what you're up to. Down here trying to get your rocks off."

David's shoulders slumped helplessly. "I don't . . ." He gave up on reason.

"You will say nothing to your mother," Pete commanded harshly.

"Okay," David said, thinking that he had never had a legitimate conversation with his mother anyway.

"I mean it! Not a damn thing!"

"All right, I won't! Even if I did, she wouldn't listen to me. I swear." He was desperately trying to soothe his father with a sense of security so as to avoid any more physical contact, but he seemed to only be making things worse.

"No, there will not be an 'even if I did!'"

"All right, I won't say anything," said David, calmly trying to hide his fear and desperation. He just wanted to get back to his room.

"Why don't I believe you?" his father asked, even more harshly. He reached for something to wield and found a large bread knife, of all incidental things.

David's eyes widened in horror, "I promise. I won't say anything," he pleaded in a high-pitched voice, wincing.

Pete reared the knife back, holding it by the blade as if ready to strike with the handle.

"I won't! I promise!"

He saw the knife come down and ducked and rolled away from between his father and the counter. The knife hit the counter and broke, cutting Pete's hand. The blade hit the floor and slid underneath the refrigerator—probably a lucky break. Pete turned and looked at his son sprawled out on the floor, eyes huge from horror and wet with tears. Both of them were panting hard. Pete started toward David.

"I told you, I won't say anything," begged David.

"I'll teach you to fuck around with me!" Pete yelled.

He grabbed David by the shirt and slapped him hard across the face. David's eyes watered more. Pete kneed him in the testicles, literally pushing them up into his stomach.

"OW!" David grunted desperately, fear and immense pain mounting.

He fell to the ground, and Pete kicked him in the ribs hard, knocking away David's breath and making him unable to yell again. Pete stood over David's writhing figure as if considering delivering another blow, but he decided against it and went back into the living room, nursing his hand with a wad of paper towels. After lying on the floor and crying nauseously for several minutes, David managed to crawl upright. He walked back into his room, lay down on the bed, and fell into a familiar, uneasy asleep.

3

David remembered this vividly as he walked into the dining room. He had made the mistake of showing resistance and autonomy to his father, and things only became worse. Why did he do it again? It was insane. That kitchen scene would surely be reenacted, but it would probably be much, much worse with his mother involved. He thought of how his father had unfairly punished him for something that he could not control: David had never asked for his father's harlot to show up then, he never wanted to hear what he heard, and he never even considered telling Janet about what his father had done. The outburst moments ago was something David actually could control, and if his parents bothered to acknowledge that simple fact, the repercussions would surely be markedly more severe. His anger mounted as he reflected on the continuous unfair treatment from both his mother and father.

Mr. and Mrs. Stewart looked at David as he entered. He quickly realized that his previous assumption about the sagacious soothsayers in movies was true.

"There is something bad about this house," Mr. Stewart whispered abruptly, obviously determined to say whatever he needed to before David's parents returned. His eyes looked scared. He reached to gently seize David's arm, as if to drive the effect of his words into David with his grip. "It tends to bring out the worst in people. Good people."

David thought that his parents had never been good people, but he said nothing. He also had a cursory, irrational jolt of worry about how much worse his punishment could be this time.

"We came to warn your parents, but they seem a little ... " he lifted his hand in the air, palm down, and tilted it minutely back and forth, indicating uncertainty.

David, for fear of them, would normally never utter a negative word about his parents to anyone, but now he approached Mr. Stewart eagerly, "Yes, sir, they are a little off. A lot off if you ask me—they're crazy!" he whispered frantically. For a fleeting second, David hoped that Mr. Stewart would leap up and come to his rescue. He suddenly felt an unexplained gratitude toward this total stranger, but before he was able to conceive the emotion, it was gone. Could this man possibly be serious? David did not have time to consider how strange this uncomfortable encounter actually was.

"Yes, well, we just wanted to warn you. If there is ever anything you need, please come over and see us right away." He seemed to know something he would not tell. "The last owners of this house didn't just move away. They were forced out."

"What—?"

Just then David's mom and dad came in. Janet was rubbing her forehead with her index finger and thumb ominously. She had her eyes closed in her typical irritated, superior demeanor. "David, will you please take the garbage out?" she said impatiently.

"Since when do I take the garbage out?" David asked, too angry that he had been interrupted to notice that she was making a valiant effort to ignore his outburst in the kitchen. This was going to get bad.

Janet froze, obviously taken aback again. "We'll talk later, Davie." She sounded as though her nerves were shot, her jaw tight and teeth clenched, her mouth for once at a loss for words at David's inexplicable rebellion.

His heart sank anew. "Okay," he sighed, and then he left, head down, possibly more frightened and confused by his cheek than his parents.

On his way out he thought more about what the Stewarts had said, but he spent little time rationalizing. Oh, how he wished that kind old man would see how mistreated he was and steal him away. He wondered—not for the first time—why his parents had never allowed anyone to adopt him. They probably got off simply making someone else's life as miserable as their own, and who better to be their punching bag than a scrawny, reserved, listless son. When he stepped out the front door, his earlier feeling of quasi-triumph had vanished completely, and he looked around, now immersed in fear of what would happen when the neighbors left. Everything seemed very different when he was alone outside, farther away from the only two people on the planet who seemed able to assist him right now. He continued to the garbage can and put the bag in.

In his room he sat in the desk chair again and looked out the window. He started to drowse again, thinking of everything he had been told downstairs. For the first time, it dawned on him that the Stewarts may be a few players short of a game of Marco-Polo, and he felt suddenly hopeless again as his fantasies of being rescued faded, but this also made him feel bad for the poor old couple. Whether soft and kindly old neighbors giving a sincere greeting or feeble-minded old Alzheimer's patients, they didn't deserve to be looked down upon and manipulated by his insincere parents.

And what was with Mr. Stewart's frantic omens? Mrs. Stewart's watery stare? How could a house bring out the worst in someone? The wall color wasn't that bad. Were they just two bored old lovers who wanted to get a kick out of messing with the new kid? Were they sadistic or just goofy? Christ, apparently everyone was out to get him.

David dreamt.

He dreamt that he was running through the woods looking for something. He didn't consciously know what he was looking for, but he knew that he was looking for something. He kept running until he passed his parents, who were both lying on the ground in a pool of blood; he barely gave them a glance. There were more important things at stake right now than the two people who had done everything in their power to make his life a living hell. Then he ran past the Stewarts' house. Mr. Stewart was also lying on the ground in a pool of blood, and David gave him more consideration than he had his own parents! Only then did David begin to feel desperate. For the second time, his hope of Mr. Stewart's being his savior was destroyed. He ran past a short kid about his own age. He wasn't wimpy, but short. The kid tried to catch up with him, but soon he fell behind, tripped, and simply lay on the ground, face down, unmoving. He ran past a girl whom he had never before seen. He slowed to get a better look at her; though inexperienced, David knew that even the most pressing of tasks can be momentarily put off for the sake of a beautiful girl. She was pretty—very pretty—although it seemed that she didn't know it, which made her seem even prettier. She had blonde hair and big, dewy blue eyes; David felt a queer sense of trite perfection. She waved at him; no pretty girl had ever so much as talked about him (but this was his dream). Even in his unconscious imagination, David's meek nature overwhelmed him, his sense of desperation and direction returned, and he didn't wave back. He shyly glanced away and just kept running, feeling a little flushed. He glanced back to see her walk away from him and approach a small group of indistinguishable people. Way to blow the sure shot, Davie. Then he ran past a small dog. He didn't know what kind of dog it was, but it looked friendly enough. It was shaggy and had light-brown hair; it just sat and stared at David as he ran closer and closer, but before David reached it, the dog had begun to lie down. Its eyes closed, and it slumped over, blood leaking from its mouth and nose. What bizarre details one notices in dreams . . . Finally, David reached something close to what he was searching for: the garbage can at the end of his driveway. It wasn't exactly the thing that he had been seeking, but it would do just as well for now. He didn't know how he knew, but he did. He stopped and sat beside it, heart racing, trying to catch his breath, this time waiting for something . . . perhaps his mother's next bag of garbage. He had unfinished business that would soon need to be dealt with.

4

David woke slowly. His room began to fade into vision, and the bright Alabama sun disoriented him as it shone through the window from a cloudless sky. He looked out and saw that the garbage he had put in yesterday was gone, as was the memory of the previous night's unnerving dream.

I wonder why you never notice the garbage men when they come to get your trash, he thought awkwardly. He was sure he had seen them before; he could picture their big vehicle, but he couldn't recount any sure image of them or any time that he had watched them work. *They just go completely unnoticed . . . like birds . . . like me.*

He got out of bed to get ready for school and went downstairs for some breakfast. His parents were, of course, still asleep. His father had no job, and his mother did various odd jobs every now and then. She never bothered mentioning to David what it was that she did, and David never bothered to ask, but he always noticed her leaving the house at strange hours. He would never dare interrogate her, because he knew what would come of that. David assumed that they sold pot or got by on money from welfare checks or something like that, just like any other smutty family. He didn't know surely though, and he didn't care to know. They had somehow acquired—or more likely, inherited—this decent, two-story house, and he still didn't know why they even chose to move here. David imagined extravagantly that they were running from someone or had to get away from something as though they were in the Witness Protection Program. Miraculously, he was even provided with essentials such as food and clothes, though both were stale and plain. His preferences were never taken into consideration, but like Baloo the Bear always said, "The bare necessities of life will come to you." He generally ate what his father ate, which usually came from a refrigerated package. He had never indulged in food, and he did not snack. He had grown accustomed to eating cheap, fatty foods as little as once a day, and his stomach no longer grumbled in protest when he went long stretches without.

He ate a bowl of stale cereal (Pete and Janet, much like small children, seemed incapable of properly storing any sort of food that came in a bag), got his backpack, and went outside to wait for the bus. He wasn't sure why a bus even came to this place. Sure, the neighborhood was quaint enough, but David thought that he was the only kid in this neighborhood that rode the bus. The subdivision was surrounded by what seemed to be a vast, dense forest, and the school was five or six miles away, down a cracked, gravelly woodland road and past a small old-fashioned town, complete with cobblestone and macadam and family-owned diners and rusty fire escapes and a rundown, foggy-glassed five-and-dime general store.

David stopped by the garbage can and sat down at the edge of his driveway. Since his parents had never bothered to take him to school, he had ridden a bus for the entire span of his education. Most mornings, with his parents still in bed and with no other way to get around, David would worry that the bus had perhaps already passed without his noticing, but now he simply sat in a non-contemplative daze. His mind a blank slate, he sat slightly slack-jawed with half-lidded eyes staring at the asphalt for well over three minutes. He slowly—though not determinedly—turned his head toward the garbage can and began tracing patterns in his mind along the many scuffs and scratches on the weathered plastic, and when the bus stopped almost directly in front of him, he didn't notice until the loud puff from the air brakes snapped him out of his trance. He got on the bus, took a seat, and scooted over to look out the window, as he often did.

Once at school, David went to his locker to get his things for first period. First, he had World History, which was by far his least favorite subject and a poor way to start each day, but he managed. On the way to his class, he saw a group of seniors storming through the hallways and pushing the ninth-graders out of their way for no other purpose than simply to make spectacles of themselves. They were, of course, loud, proud, brash, right wing Southern stereotypes, every one. Most classic rednecks that David knew of were egotistic and biased and prejudiced, and he could nearly always predict the extent of their accents based upon how known they made their presence, a skill that made him smile inside despite its judgmental basis.

The day went by uneventfully until just after lunch. At his locker David watched as a small ninth-grader had an accidental collision with the awkwardly positioned leg of a complacent junior who had been leaning against the wall. The older kid had a few friends with him, and he apparently decided that he needed to be showy, so he turned and pushed the small kid into a locker, acting as though the kid had tried to get away with clipping his leg. His friends all hushed and grinned, hoping for some excitement.

The freshman looked familiar to David. He was small, but not necessarily wimpy. He had brown hair and average wire-rimmed glasses, and he seemed a little like David himself, reserved and quiet. While David was not so composed as to interfere, he stopped gathering his belongings, tilted his head reflectively, and watched the kid intently, struggling to identify the familiarity of his demeanor. He did not even notice that he was staring uninhibited and alone at the scene before him.

"You might wanna watch where you're goin' next time, kid," the older guy said loudly, grinning at his friend.

"Okay, I'm sorry," the kid managed, trying hard to not look him in the eye.

"Aw, look at the little baby, he's sorry!" the big guy yelled this time. There was no compromise with these people. "Stay outta the way, you little queer, or you're gonna get yourself beat to shit." Did he really just say that out loud?

The kid turned and hurried away toward David, whose gaze continued to follow the kid as he approached.

"Hey! What are y'all lookin' at?" Now the bigger guy was yelling accusingly through the hallway toward David, who looked around trying to figure out just who "y'all" actually was.

"I—" David blinked confusedly as the awareness of his own existence returned. He shook his head to indicate that he had no response. The jerk and his friends all laughed and turned away, seeming rather content at the way David had made himself seem like any other mongoloid who would sit by and hold his tongue while they had their way.

"But that's exactly what I am," he mumbled to himself as the kid tripped over his foot in a frantic effort to escape the wrath of the high-school horror.

"Sorry," the kid said. "I'm sorry." He raised his voice shrilly.

"No, it's fine." David looked away from the retreating bumpkins and grabbed the boy's shoulder to steady him. "If I didn't want to be touched, I wouldn't come out in public. Those guys are jerks, don't worry about them," but the kid had already scurried on his way down the hall.

David sighed as he watched the semblance of himself rush through the crowded hall, broken, beaten, and criticized into submission, left only to skitter past all the faces that always seemed to be disdainfully jeering at him. Witnessing an act of depraved sadism from this new perspective made David more aware than ever of how utterly pathetic he must seem. He gathered the rest of his belongings and made his way quietly through the hallway. Maybe most of these people weren't that bad. Looking around in this new light—almost a spectator of himself—David thought that most of these people probably didn't judge him at all; most of them didn't even seem to notice him.

Later, just after his lunch period, David arrived at his algebra class with a few minutes to kill, so he sat down in the cold chair and looked around the dimly lit room. The teacher, who had plans to spend the next ninety minutes in almost complete darkness lecturing about linear equations and quadratic formulas while the eyes of thirty kids flocked to the projector screen—the only light in the room—like moths, didn't even bother turning the overhead light on between classes. The students, their meals just beginning to settle and their brains just begging to power down, all chatted mutedly with unexcited, half-lidded eyes. David looked at all the posters on the wall and managed to absorb not a single message: "Order of Operations: Please Excuse My Dear Aunt Sally;" "Study Skills;" "Test-Taking Tips;" "Hang in There," with a picture of a bear falling out of a tree; "Stay Afloat," with a picture of a sailboat; "Reading is Cool," with a cartoon penguin carrying a book; "Math is the New English," with a cartoon of Einstein and Newton deep in conversation, filling chat-bubbles with mathematical numbers and symbols; a pyramid of prime numbers; an entire poster tracking the value of Pi to probably the sixty-eighth decimal place . . .

The bell finally rang and startled David out of his daze. His mind was uncharacteristically remote, and he hadn't even noticed as nearly sixteen sleepy kids filed in the doorway in the last few moments before the bell's ring and filled the remaining empty seats around him. Even when the teacher came in and began monotonously droning about algebraic functions, David couldn't focus enough to take notes; he just glanced around the room at all the dimly lit faces of his peers and wondered how many of them were neutral (as he had come to think of them) when it came to people like himself. He thought that few of his classmates would be eager to torment freshmen in the fashion that he'd witnessed earlier, but then again, none of them had any easy targets that were three or four years younger. David doubted, though, that many of them would leap at the opportunity to stand up for someone being harassed by a group of older students. For the first time in his life, David found himself disdainful of The Neutrals merely for their lack of involvement, and the hypocrisy of this notion made his wavering faith in himself and in humanity as a whole falter even more severely.

After full minutes of pessimistically scanning the classroom, scorning the world, and slighting himself, David's thoughts inevitably came to his parents. Self-pitying thoughts of his living situation led David, for the first time all day, to ponder their strange visitors from the day before. After sleeping all night and carrying on today, the whole encounter seemed surreal, and the actual conversation he'd had with Mr. Stewart seemed laughable at best. The fact that his parents hadn't stormed his bedroom, seized him in his slumber, and tossed his limp body down the stairs after the Stewarts left made David's memory of the event even less compelling.

When David took a break from pondering the lunacy of the previous day, he glanced at the clock and was surprised to find that class was nearly halfway over, and he had still not written a single word, letter, or number in his notebook. He finally dated his notes, as his anal nature always forced him to do, and struggled to blindly situate himself in the context of his teacher's rant, but he still could not get his head in the game. Soon he was staring at the clock again and wondering how the erratic second-hand was actually serving any purpose overall. It was straight up, on the twelve, and after about seven extremely large and irregular ticks, it was straight down, on the six; from here it took about fifty seconds to make it back up to the twelve. David watched this for four full rotations before even realizing what he was doing, and even then he had trouble tearing his eyes away from the clock and focusing on the Pythagorean theorem.

When the class finally ended, David hurried to his next class determined not to lose focus again. English tended to be a bit more involved than algebra anyway. When the initial bell rang and class began, however, David found himself peering around the room again; the fresh batch of faces rekindled all his old musings in a different light. He scanned the room again and again until he finally noticed the small kid with brown hair and glasses that had had the run-in by the locker area. His squirrelly frame sitting quietly in the front corner of the room struck in David a familiarity and fondness that bordered on irrational. His mind wandered again, and for the next forty minutes, he was not able to focus on his class work at all. His last class of the day went the same.

On the bus David noticed the squirrelly kid for the third time and had to fight an uncharacteristic compulsion to sit next to him and strike up a conversation. Instead he sat in an empty seat and gazed out the window at the passing trees, too distracted to be apprehensive about his return home until the bus turned onto his street. When his house was in sight, a familiar knot tightened in his stomach and his flesh turned cold, though his core was hot and feverish. He got up rigidly and walked to the front of the bus, realizing that he hadn't even noticed when the kid got off the bus, and exited the bus at his driveway.

He stepped inside his house and slowly and quietly closed the front door in hopes that neither parent would notice his arrival. He crossed the kitchen, saw no one in the hallway, and made it halfway up the stairs before he heard his mother threateningly clear her throat. He froze.

"Just who in the fiery hell do you think you are?" she demanded, walking around the corner and into view. But when David could think of no reply, her pitch went up until she sounded shrill and frantic. He had quite likely never before directly rendered her this pissed-off. "You have done a lot to embarrass us over the years, but I have never been so ashamed to call you my son!" Just like her, skirting around the real issue and making David seem like a shameful waste of space.

She continued screeching and swearing at the motionless David, still standing halfway up the stairs and looking docilely at his feet, for nearly a full minute, and just when David thought he could take no more, Pete roared an interruption from the living room, "Will you shut your fucking face!"

Janet stopped mid-sentence and froze with her mouth open, looking incredulous, but she didn't falter long. "Come in here and deal with him, honey!" she called, as if David were the object of his father's humble request. David's heart hastened just the same, and he looked up terrified from his shoes and opened his mouth to protest, but no words would come out. He had known this was coming; deep down, he had known all along. Of course his mother would never hit him; in her demented reality, she was still a dainty lady, and dainty ladies do not hit their children. They call upon their husbands to do it.

Pete grunted and grumbled and swore as he heaved himself out of the recliner and stomped moodily to the stairwell, obviously holding every lost second against David. "You've got some damn nerve talking to your mother like you know what's what! She ought to beat you within an inch of your life herself."

His voice was loud and brash and hateful and every bit as condescending and sanctimonious as the seniors' and juniors' at David's Alabama public high school. For a brief moment, David envisioned his redfaced father by the lockers in his high school, dragging a pitiful freshman down the hallway by his shirt collar, roaring threats and curses all the while to draw in more attention.

"Are you gonna talk, son, or you gonna stand there all day with your thumb up your ass and that stupid pout on your face?" Pete began yelling even louder as he mounted the stairs and approached David, whose inconvenient daydream was instantly shattered. Despite himself, David took an instinctive step backwards, up the stairs, in an attempt to avoid his father's swinging, meaty palm, but he knew this only made Pete enjoy what was coming even more.

Pete grabbed him by the nape of the neck and thrust his bulky arm backward and downward, thrusting David's torso toward the floor below. In an instant David's feet were above his head, and he pulled both arms forward to brace himself for contact with the floor. Both palms slammed into the ground at the same time, and his first sensation was, with such clarity, a stinging burn from the impact with the carpet. Next his chin and chest hit the floor at approximately the same instant, his feet still in the air, and his entire body bounced inches off the ground as all of his breath was thrust hoarsely out of his lungs at once and his chin stung with the same carpet burn he'd gotten on his palms.

David lay still on the floor groaning and rasping in an attempt to refill his lungs with air, and he was vaguely aware of his mother's smug figure standing in the doorway with her arms crossed, watching contentedly. Pete bumbled down the stairs to ground level, and before David could even nurse his throbbing wrists, he was kicked bluntly in the gut, making his efforts to retain oxygen all the more futile. He threw his head back and tried to yell, but no sound would come out. He could draw air neither in nor out of his mouth, which opened and closed like that of a dying fish. Pete kicked again and again, and David forced himself to roll over so that his hips and ribs took most of the blows from his assailant. Though they would be severely bruised the next day, his new position allowed David to at least begin breathing regularly again, though his throat was raw and sore due to such a large quantity of air being forced through it in one instant.

David lay on the floor accepting Pete's kicks and screams for the next two or three minutes. Though he could scarcely bear the pain, he could do nothing in the way of moving or fleeing at this point, and he was somewhat relieved that his brain was still getting oxygen. He squeezed his eyes shut tighter with each blow, and fresh, hot tears squirted through his closed eyes with the force of every kick.

When Pete was finally worn out and Janet was finally satisfied, they both walked away without another word and left David to drag his battered body up the stairs. He knew that he had better be well away from the area when either of them happened to pass back through.

5

After a miserable evening and night of gingerly rolling about restlessly in his bed, David awoke to the fall's morning rays of sun shining through his bedroom window. He never set an alarm because he was almost always in bed by full dusk, and he had never in his life slept past eight a.m. This morning he saw that he had only about twenty minutes to get showered and catch the bus.

Looking in his mirror, David was relieved to see that the carpet burn on his chin was now only a faint red rash and the skin had not been broken. Also, his father hadn't managed to hit or kick David's face, so hadn't left any noticeable scrapes or bruises. The only marks were on his ribs, back, and stomach. He realized that his concern was likely in vain; adults, despite their preachy speeches, were often quite as incapable of taking action against an obvious injustice as a Neutral in the hallway. They generally showed superfluous concern that fell short of any emotion compelling enough to spur one into action.

Once on the bus, David noticed the same kid already in his same seat on the bus, but this morning David was too exhausted to have an urge to speak to him today. He just wanted to get a good night's rest and have his ribs stop throbbing and get his thoughts back on track and be able to concentrate in class again.

The day was pretty grueling for David, and he found himself relieved that the weekend was so near and that he could spend two days at home in his room; he planned to sleep for longer than he had in his entire life. He struggled to get through his first two classes without falling out of his chair in a dead sleep on the floor, and he spent third period clutching at his abdomen trying to differentiate the severe hunger pangs due to his lack of dinner from the searing throbs due to his beating. After lunch David's algebra class was spent in much the same fashion as the first two classes of the day; his lunch, settling and soothing his aching stomach, allowed him to once again focus on how desperately exhausted he was. Near the end of class, he realized that he had forgotten his books for English and would have to rush back to his locker between classes.

When the bell rang, he struggled to hurry through the hall while nursing his wounds and moving in a way that would cause them minimal pain. He got to his locker and retrieved his needed books, but when he turned around, he stopped to observe one of the older students slap the belongings out of the kid's hands and onto the floor. He then shoved the kid into the lockers and loudly said, "Careful!" in mock-concern. His buddies chortled and nudged him to signal a casually approaching teacher, and the older kids all just continued on their way. The teacher passed as the kid was scrambling to pick up his fallen notebooks and glanced down wordlessly in momentary amusement before continuing down the hall.

David thought of his contempt for all The Neutrals who refused to stand up for someone in need, all the adults who complained about the problems of bullying and yet did nothing to prevent or remedy the problem. What went on in this school wasn't even bullying. David thought that bullying should be somewhat random, but these people were just so filled with hate and insecurities, and their perceptions of what is fun had been so severely skewed that it made David want to vomit. He decided that, even if he was too weaselly to risk getting shoved or smacked in the gut today, the kid could at least use some sympathy. He quick-stepped forward to assist in picking up the scattered books that all the other students were obliviously stepping all over and kicking across the tiled halls.

"Butterfingers," he muttered, trying to ease the tension as he handed the kid a stack of scattered papers. The kid took them from David without glancing up or saying a word.

"You should have held him off a few more seconds, then maybe that teacher would have had a better excuse not to ignore you." When the kid neither smiled nor nodded nor acknowledged David's presence at all, he worried that he might be coming off as a jerk.

"Don't worry too much. He probably just didn't see you in the shade of his towering ego." Finding a common enemy is the best way to make friends, right?

The kid finally laughed, perhaps a little too heartily. "Yeah, the teacher or the junior?" He stopped scrambling to retrieve his belongings and looked at David for the first time.

David smiled and extended his hand to be shaken. "I'm David. What's your name?"

"My name's Jess," he said as he took David's hand and lightly shook it.

"Oh, Jess," David smiled again, trying to urge the kid to chat. "What class do you have next?" he asked, though he already knew the answer.

"English," Jess replied.

"Hey, I do too." He felt like an actor just reciting lines, but if it got this kid to open up, maybe it would be worth it. "Do you want to walk with me?"

"Sure," Jess said, suddenly sounding eager, and they started off together down the hall.

Wow, the third day of school and I already have a friend, David thought, secretly as excited as Jess appeared to be. *That has got to be a record. Maybe this stupid new city could be the turning-over of a new leaf.*

They walked in a somewhat uncomfortable silence, as David had exhausted the extent of his casually forced conversation and Jess did not seem concerned with making small talk. Once in the classroom, Jess took his usual seat in the front corner, and David scanned the nearly full room for an empty seat. "I'll see you later," he said to Jess before heading to the other side of the room. Finally his aching gut was calming down and he didn't feel as sleepy as he had been feeling. He was even able to concentrate a little better on the class work. It seemed for now that he may have found a way to finally deal with his insecurities and set his mind at ease.

After English, David caught up with Jess and struck up another conversation about what classes they each had last period, and before splitting David suggested that they would see each other on the bus after school.

In his last class of the day, David finally felt that things were gaining a sense of normalcy again, and the effects of the past few hectic days were wearing off. He was able to concentrate on taking notes without dwelling too much on anything at all, and he actually looked forward to the bus ride to come, during which he and Jess would trade opinions on the best and worst teachers so far in high school and the easiest and hardest classes, and David would discover that Jess lived only two or three blocks away in his neighborhood.

"Mrs. Harrison is easily the most frightening teacher I've ever had," Jess opined, "and her Biweekly Polynomial Blitz exercises are the most stressful things you could be forced to do." David chuckled at the accuracy of Jess's declaration. "Well, this is where I get off. I'll see you Monday."

David was surprised to realize that they were already in his neighborhood, Thriftson Hills. It felt as though they had been riding less than ten minutes, but it had already been nearly forty. He glanced around at the houses to fixate himself in his cognitive map of the neighborhood and was about to announce that he lived just around the corner, but Jess was already trotting gaily off the bus. David thought that he looked completely at ease and oblivious to all around him, and he wondered if Jess was always so unconcerned—despite his being a bit of a social leper—or if his own efforts had had a positive effect on Jess's demeanor. He decided that he would make an effort to hang out with Jess outside of school next week. God knew he didn't have any other obligations.

The weekend passed uneventfully for David. He managed to stay unnoticed in his bedroom reading books and catching up on sleep all weekend. He would quietly go downstairs to get food whenever he noticed his mother's car leaving the driveway; this almost always meant that Pete would be unconscious in his recliner.

On Sunday, as usual, David felt a gentle excitement at getting away from his house and parents and returning to school again the next day, but this time he was slightly more excited because he would get to see Jess. He was already getting a bit flustered and nervous to invite Jess to do something after school; he felt as though he were preparing to ask a beautiful girl on a first date. He thought this somewhat strange, but he had never really spent genuine time with anyone, never had a legitimate conversation with a peer, and never actually requested anyone's company in a social setting. Truthfully he wasn't even sure what normal kids expected when it came to friendships. Would Jess think him weird for extending an invitation so hastily? Or would he think David insincere if he didn't start getting more proactive? Making friends shouldn't be this stressful. No wonder David had never done it before.

Monday morning, when David got on the bus, he sat with Jess in his seat at the front of the bus and feigned a sleepy, subdued greeting. Jess, however, seemed perky enough, and he immediately began talking about his first class of the day. "Hey! Did you have a nice weekend? I was doing homework last night, and I can't wait for Mr. Wilson's physical science class. Did you get to see his presentation with that old light bulb? He got it to light up with just like a glass of salt water!"

"No," David glumly, "I have Mrs. Peters. She just lectures straight from her PowerPoints the entire class. Besides, I have Mr. Mooring's world history class first period. More like Mr. Booring." Jess laughed heartily at that, and his giddiness got David chuckling too, despite his boring lineup of teachers this year.

They continued discussing their different homework assignments and teacher presentations and yearlong projects for the duration of the bus ride, and once at school they agreed to meet outside the cafeteria to have lunch together and then went their separate ways.

David's apprehension slightly wore off over the course of the day, but by the time he and Jess were back on the bus and he was preparing to set himself up for either supreme disappointment or contentment, he began getting a little nervous again. He made small talk for the duration of the bus ride, but when they turned into Marlboro Hills, he knew that he had to say something soon.

"Hey, you know, you should come over to my house some time." David said, convincing himself that he felt bold, yet feeling naturally skeptical about Jess's sincerity. He worried that if he didn't make clear his desire to be a real friend that Jess might soon dismiss him.

"Sure," Jess said eagerly, perhaps a bit too eagerly, but David really didn't notice. "I'd like that."

"Good, good," David nodded, smiling, now unsure of what to say next. He finally broke the awkward silence as Jess was preparing to dismount the bus. "I'll see you tomorrow then."

Jess's gratitude seemed to flow out of every pore in his body, and it made David's heart ache for the poor kid. After fifteen years of self-pity, he had finally met someone who seemed even more pathetic than he was, and the brutal reality of it suddenly hit him hard.

For the next few days, David and Jess carried on their routine, greeting each other on the bus each morning, eating lunch together, and saying goodbye on the bus each afternoon, and, each day, David was pleased to find that Jess still seemed unyieldingly excited to see him. They sometimes walked to their math class and to their bus together in awkward silence, and they sometimes ate lunch without saying a word, but neither seemed to care. Both undoubtedly had strong opinions on several issues but had little motivation to voice them. They talked occasionally about trivial subjects such as the previous day's homework assignments or an upcoming test, but they never volunteered personal information to one another. David was grateful nonetheless to have found a friend, and he never once questioned the validity of what he had thus deemed his friendship; not only did he refuse to believe that he had chosen Jess as a friend for the wrong reasons, but he never even took the time to conjure the thought. He was too caught up in the newfound excitement of each day to entertain the notion that Jess's appeal may have sprung solely from his many similarities with David. David had decided on a subconscious level never to acknowledge the fact that he had piteously befriended himself or someone in an even worse situation, someone whom he could help in a way that may ultimately serve to help himself. He never stressed about these possibilities, and perhaps that was for the better. Perhaps that is the essence of true friendship.

6

One day, after breezing through an English test that brightened David's whole demeanor, he decided to finally attempt to extend another invitation to Jess. The two together had thus far acted more like vaguely familiar lab partners than friends, and while David would offer no complaint about their engagements, he felt optimistic enough to try to have fun for the first time in his life.

Just before departing for their next class, David offered another nonchalant invitation. "Oh, hey, a few days ago, I mentioned that you could come over to my house or something if you wanted, and I just wanted to let you know that I don't have any plans any time soon, so you can just let me know if you want to do something."

Jess's desperation was painted all over his face. "Yeah! I can come today! My parents don't really care where I go." He paused, looking embarrassed. "Well, if that's not a problem, I mean . . ." It was more a question than a statement.

David could see why many people may not immediately take to Jess, yet he sadly took notice for the fifth or sixth time of the many similarities between the two of them. He was mildly surprised by Jess's response but pleased nonetheless. "Yeah, you may as well," he shrugged and grinned. "My parents would probably just ignore me if I asked for permission anyway. I'd be willing to bet that they wouldn't even notice the two of us there." For a moment he became worried that Jess would be turned off by their behavior, but the concern was fleeting. He had come to find comfort in Jess's sincerity. "You'll have to excuse them, though. They really are kind of . . . crazy," he concluded almost apologetically.

Apparently unfazed, Jess said, "Okay, I can do that!"

"Good. I'll see you on the bus then." David smiled in spite of himself as Jess turned away and rushed clumsily to his last class.

In Mrs. Peters' physical science class, David diligently transcribed the notes from the projector screen to his notebook, but he absorbed absolutely none of the information that was being taught. His mind was whirring, computing, and considering things completely unrelated to the three (or was it four?) states of matter. He began panicking once again about whether or not Jess would be impressed with what David had to offer. Granted, Jess likely wouldn't be impressed per se, but would he ever want to come back? Would he even still enjoy David's company after today? What on earth would David do to entertain a guest? He could scarcely entertain himself without napping or staring at something mundane. Sure, books were great to kill some time, but he couldn't imagine that they would be an interesting conversation piece among friends.

By the time the bell rang to dismiss students for the afternoon, David's apprehension was palpable. His mouth was dry with a copper-like taste, his head was swimming slightly, and his entire body was lightly coated with cool perspiration. He suddenly felt sleepy and couldn't keep himself from yawning every minute or so; he wished now that he hadn't invited Jess after all so he could just go home and sleep.

And yet, here was an excited-looking Jess scurrying clumsily down the hallway toward David as he headed toward the buses. In light of his newfound friendship, David was terribly concerned about meeting swift disappointment if Jess made an about-face and decided that David wasn't worth his time. As Jess closed in on him in the hall, David convinced himself that everything would be fine. The two of them got along fine on the bus and at lunch, sometimes sitting for ten or fifteen minutes in complete silence. They both understood that they could get by without always making small talk, and other times they managed to find some common interests to discuss. Who knew, maybe Jess liked to read, too. The two of them could sit around all afternoon, and discussions of Mr. Mooring and Mrs. Williams would shift to topics of David's tattered old copies of *Huckleberry Finn* and *Sherlock Holmes*.

"Hey, David!" Jess said gleefully. "How was science?"

David felt better already. "Hey. It was typical. Just a ton of notes like usual."

"Oh, that's too bad."

"Yeah, so don't even tell me about all the demonstrations you got in Mr. Wilson's class this morning," David teased.

Jess grinned contentedly. "It really is a shame that you didn't get better teachers." They got on the bus and sat in their usual seat together, and David proceeded to learn about physical science through Jess's extensive descriptions of Mr. Wilson's fantastic-sounding demonstrations.

As the bus neared Jess's stop, they informed the driver that he would be getting off at David's house, and David's heart sank when the driver insisted that they needed a signed note from a parent for him to allow someone off at a different stop. How would David ever convince his parents to sign something like that? But then he remembered that he lived less than three blocks away, and he wondered why he hadn't mentioned it before.

"It's all right, Jess. Just walk down the block to Jade Street there, and turn right. I live just down the road, so you'll see me walking back toward you."

"Oh, you live in this neighborhood too?" Jess asked excitedly. "Why didn't you tell me before?" David felt very flattered that Jess was excited to discover that he lived so close and apparently would have liked to have known sooner, but he found himself at a loss for words. He just grinned and stared at Jess.

"I—" the air brakes hissed, and David was spared looking goofy for too long.

"I'll see you in a minute!" Jess snatched his belongings and hopped gaily off the bus. David felt a fleeting sense of embarrassment at the way Jess was obviously struggling to refrain from sprinting alongside the bus, and the back of his neck turned hot as he realized that everyone on the bus behind him was probably watching their interactions, listening to their arrangements, and judging him because of Jess's inelegance. This quickly passed, however, and the burning at the base of his neck turned into the heat of anger: anger at himself for letting such a thought even pass through his mind. Jess and he had shown each other kindness, and that alone was more than any one of the people behind him who may or may not be judging him could say.

The bus turned right onto Jade Street and bounced to a stop at the first stop sign before continuing on to David's driveway. He climbed down the bus's awkward stairs and saw that his garbage can had been knocked over into his yard. He set his bag down in the grass and heaved the heavy cart with one broken wheel back upright at the corner of his drive. By the time he looked back up the street, Jess had just turned the corner, and David trotted off toward him.

"Man! Good thing you live so close. I can't believe that guy wouldn't just let me get off with you," Jess announced when David was within speaking distance.

"Yeah, lucky," David mused.

They caught up with each other, and David turned back to walk alongside Jess toward the house. Jess finally asked the dreaded question: "So what do you want to do?"

David truly had no idea what to say at this point. "I don't really know. I kind of just realized that there's not that much to do at my house." He frowned slightly, "Sorry."

"That's ok," Jess said, unperturbed. "I don't do anything either except read comic books and watch movies."

"Oh, wow, that's cool. I've never read any comic books. Do you have a lot?"

"Yeah! My grandmother sends me a few every year, and on my birthdays or Christmas she sometimes sends five or six!" Jess spoke quickly and gleefully. His excitement at the tiniest of things made David grateful, because it took so much pressure off him to think of good conversation topics. And despite Jess's gaucheness, David was starting to think that Jess might be more interesting and fun-loving than himself.

"That's awesome. I read a lot of books, but I don't really watch movies or read comics." He laughed humorlessly, "I don't even own a single movie."

David noticed that Jess had glanced ahead nervously and wondered if his admissions were putting Jess off, but Jess continued talking animatedly nonetheless. "Wow, you're missing out! I own like thirty or forty DVDs, and my grandmother sent me a little TV with a built-in player. I like to read and all, but sometimes it's nice to watch it all play out instead of making it up in your head. And a good comic book is sometimes just as good as reading a book." He glanced at David's book bag in the lawn and then his eyes darted with concern toward the house.

David tried to ignore his uneasiness and carry on the conversation. "I've always been curious about Superman. He's such an icon and all. I've just never seen any of it."

Jess perked up again without hesitation, as if nothing had been wrong, "Superman! I have like fifty Superman comics. He's my favorite . . ." His voice trailed off. "Of course I have all the movies too."

They had reached David's driveway, and he bent to pick up his bag. Jess continued walking along the sidewalk, and when he saw that David had stopped, he looked at the house one last time, and his eyes widened in disbelieving horror. David looked at his house. It looked the same as when he had left it. "What? Is something wrong?" he asked.

"No," Jess said, gulping, obviously trying to convince himself that this were true. "I'm just not used to being so close to that house." He paused uneasily. "It's an old story. A dumb story . . . sort of like a legend, I guess."

David thought of his odd visitors just a few days ago, thought of how he had snapped at his mother and father with much less provocation than they had given him in the past, remembered Mr. Stewart saying, "It tends to bring out the worst in people. Good people." But he opted not to inquire about the legend, feeling a bit resentful. He started toward the front door.

"I'm not going in it," Jess said, still standing on the sidewalk where he had stopped. He laughed humorlessly in a vain attempt to make the statement sound less uppity.

"Why not? That's my house."

"That's Mr. Batterman's house. Mr. Batterman built it way before I was born, and he was crazy. He died a few years ago in the mental hospital down in Mulberry."

David was thoroughly confused. "So it's not his house anymore."

"No, that's not what I mean," Jess said. "That house is evil."

David swallowed hard as he pushed thoughts of Mr. Stewart and his parents away. "Well, I live there. Look at me: I'm fine."

"Yeah, but . . . " Jess was shifting nervously. He looked supremely uncomfortable, "But maybe . . . " he paused, searching for words to say. "Well, I just don't want to go in there again. I went in once a long time ago because I was curious, and I felt different while I was inside. I swore I'd never do it again."

"Okay," David began, at an utter loss for suggestions. "Well . . ."

"It's all right," Jess said. "I better get home anyway. I have a lot of homework to get started on, now that I think about it."

"Oh," David's heart sank.

"I'll see you tomorrow, then."

"Yeah," David was starting to feel nauseous with disappointment. "Tomorrow."

"Yeah, bye." Jess turned and hurried along the sidewalk back toward his house.

David stood watching and cursing his idiocy for ever getting his hopes up. On one hand, he hadn't had to worry about entertaining a guest, but on the other, Jess hadn't even given him the opportunity to entertain him. Just hightailed it home like an immature, superstitious little schoolgirl! David started feeling bitter at Jess for reacting the way he did, and he continued wondering confusedly what exactly had just gone wrong.

He looked at his house again; it looked just like all the other houses on the street. Being so new to this neighborhood, David wondered how Jess had even discerned this house as being that of the late Mr. Batterman. He was not yet familiar with the signature characteristics of this house, the ones school kids told their little siblings to look for on "the house on Jade Street in Marlboro Hills." The foggy scar on the top left corner of the tiny attic window, the out-of-place fresh layer of paint over just the railing of the small front porch, the round stained-glass window above the garage door, the birdlike shapes carved at the top of the posts holding the awning over the porch. All these subtle characteristics eluded David, who currently had no reason to acknowledge their existence.

He stood and watched Jess hurrying out of sight. Just before he made it to the corner, he tripped and fell down. David laughed in spite of himself. It wasn't a "ha-ha, you fell" laugh, it was more like, "Sorry, I can't help but laugh." Then David realized that it was the third time he'd seen Jess trip this week. No, wait—the second. Or was it the third? He was sure it was the third. Once at school, when he tripped over that jerk's leg in the hallway. Then here, just now. But there was another time before he tripped in the hallway. What was he thinking? He didn't even know Jess before that day.

Then he remembered the dream. How could he have dreamt about someone whom he had never met? After worrying for a minute, he decided that the dream was far too vague for him to rightly decide that it had been about Jess. It was just a coincidence. Déjà vu.

He finally resigned himself to walking inside, going upstairs, and doing some homework too, though he doubted if he could concentrate knowing that his first and only friend in this new town had just blatantly ditched him. But when he got to the front door, he hesitated before stepping inside, considering what Jess and Mr. Stewart had said. As he entered, he made a conscious effort to notice any change that occurred. He stopped immediately inside the door and struggled to find any sort of internal shift, but he merely felt a little more stressed. He shook his head, as if to recollect himself, and started walking again, wondering what could be going on that would make Jess share the same sentiments as a frail old man.

When he was in the middle of the kitchen, he glanced up and saw that there were three full bags of trash leaning against the wall waiting for him. Garbage day was almost here, and Janet meant to make it count.

7

The next morning a tired and brooding David sat waiting for the bus and wondering whether Jess would even acknowledge him, or if they were even still friends.

When the bus arrived, David stood up and decided that he would just sit in his own seat today and see if Jess decided to make a move. David had made all the advancements thus far, and it wasn't fair for Jess to ditch him and then expect David to come crawling back. He climbed the steps, and his eyes almost involuntarily went straight to Jess's seat. He was surprised to find that Jess was grinning and looking at him eagerly, as if nothing out of the ordinary had happened the previous afternoon. This was a good enough signal for David, and he sat down beside Jess, as usual.

"I brought you something," Jess immediately started, struggling with his enthusiasm. This made David's stomach feel odd too; no one had ever "brought him something," and he felt a mixture of excitement, gratitude, and a little fear. Jess reached into his book bag and pulled out an extremely faded and worn comic book that was stored in a clear plastic sleeve. "It's *Action Comics No. 1*," Jess continued. "The very first appearance of Superman from the 1930s!"

"Wow." David didn't know what else to say. It was such a small act of kindness, and yet no one had ever shown him anything like it. The gravity of it nearly brought him to tears.

"There are ten stories in it, and the others are pretty good, but the Superman one tells about how he came to be the way he is. You should read it if you have time. If you like it, maybe you could borrow some of my other ones."

"You mean, I can take it out of the sleeve?"

Jess laughed, "Of course you can. How else could you read it?" David smiled nervously at that, and Jess said, "Don't worry, I know you won't hurt it. It's just a comic. I mean, it is worth a lot, because this one is so old—"

"How much is it worth?" David asked.

Jess considered, "Um, it's worth, like, thousands. My grandma sends them to me because my grandpa used to be a huge collector," he paused reflectively. "And my dad was never a fan." He paused again, regaining steam. "But I know you'll take care of it."

David grinned, completely flattered that someone would trust him with such an old, collectible item, but he still couldn't think of anything to say. He felt immensely grateful for Jess's kindness and sincerity.

"Look," Jess continued, "If you're going to read the comics, you may as well at least get the intro! I don't have all of them, but this one is important."

"You got it. I'll look it over tonight."

Jess beamed and said, "I'm sure you'll like it." For the rest of the bus ride, he gave David brief summaries of some of the adventures he would soon observe if he decided to continue reading comics about Superman. By the time they got to school, Jess had suggested that David come over soon and check out his comic collection, and David agreed to come over that very afternoon as soon as he finished all his homework and finished looking over the comic. When they got off the bus and began walking to their lockers, David had completely forgotten about the incident the previous afternoon, and was again looking forward to spending an afternoon with Jess.

When they got to the wider hallway where lockers were, David saw the familiar group of juniors and seniors, and he glanced up to catch one of the older members of the group smiling maliciously as he looked up and down Jess's squirmy form, from his generic, dirty shoes to his disheveled, somewhat oily hair. Just after they passed, David heard someone say, "Look, y'all. The tar-baby's got him a boyfriend." He glanced at Jess, who, still smiling absently, apparently hadn't heard the jab.

They got their books from their lockers and each went to their first class, and the day wore on as usual until just after lunch. The two were walking back to their lockers together from the cafeteria when David saw the group of older students walking toward them and checking them out. He turned his attention from them in hopes that they wouldn't say anything if he didn't make eye contact, and he tried to make small talk to distract Jess as well as himself, but it was to no avail.

"Hey, lovebirds," the usual instigator said snidely as he swatted the books from Jess's hands. He reached up to swipe at David's books too, but David instinctively took a step backward. The guy's friends all scoffed, but it was obvious that he was taken aback and furious that he had swung at David's hands and missed in front of all of his spectators. In an instant he lunged forward and elbowed David in the sternum, knocking him back against the lockers as his books fell to the ground after all. "Ooh, careful there, faggot." The guys all chortled and continued down the hall as David slid down the lockers to a seated position, gasping for breath.

"Are you okay?" Jess asked, gathering up both his and David's books. David nodded, grimacing. The other students in the hall just carried on with their business. Some Neutrals hardly spared them a glance while others chuckled at their expense. "I've learned that it's easier to just take their crap," Jess sighed.

"Ridiculous," David managed, but he realized that, despite the times he took pity on Jess and thought him such an incompetent runt, Jess had been right all along. Jess knew that it was easier to just put up with it than to resist and make things worse. While it made him look like a social retard, it spared him more unnecessary misery. These people could surely make his life infinitely miserable, and David understood that Jess could rightfully claim every passive defeat as a victory of sorts.

That afternoon on the bus, David listened contentedly as Jess rambled on, excited about introducing David to his comic book collection. Before the bus got to Marlboro Hills, Jess wrote down his phone number for David to call when he was ready to head over. This made David realize that he didn't even know the phone number at his new house. Given that his parents rarely took phone calls, he was willing to bet that they didn't know the number either.

After Jess dismounted the bus and it turned the corner onto Jade Street, David stood up in preparation to get off, and he noticed a man in a jumpsuit tossing the empty garbage can back to the end of his driveway. The man hopped nimbly back onto the back of the garbage truck, gripped the handle that he held to maintain his balance, and rapped his fist sharply on the side of the truck to signal the driver to drive away. David thought it strange to notice the garbage truck at his house at precisely the time his bus arrived at nearly four o'clock on a Tuesday afternoon. He thought it even stranger, however, when the garbage truck drove away from his house, continued on down the street, and turned out of sight without stopping at any other house. They must have missed his house that morning, David decided. He had no idea whether they routinely backtracked to make up for something like that, but he imagined that an irate Janet could persuade anyone to do just about anything, even over the phone.

When he got off the bus and went into his kitchen, he quietly sifted through piles of mail and bills on the kitchen counter until he found a bill that included the phone number as well as the new house's address. He quickly wrote this down to give to Jess and hurried upstairs to spend the next two hours doing homework and perusing *Action Comics No. 1.* He was not surprised to find that the first ten pages of "Superman" had him wholly captivated, and as soon as he finished with the entire comic, he snuck back downstairs to call Jess.

For the rest of the evening, David and Jess sat in Jess's bedroom and browsed through more than forty comics featuring Superman, and this didn't even tap a quarter of Jess's collection. David returned to Jess's house every afternoon that week, and by Friday he had borrowed and read upwards of fifteen comic books. For the first time in his life, David felt genuinely happy and excited every morning upon waking. His world was dramatically opening up, and when he and Jess watched the very first grainy Superman movie on Jess's tiny television, he could not have imagined a more thrilling experience.

8

Late Saturday morning, when David was sitting in the empty kitchen eating a bowl of stale Cheerios, he was startled by the unfamiliar sound of a ringing phone. He froze, and after the first ring, the tone echoed throughout the dark, silent house. When it began to ring a second time, he looked around uneasily for the phone, and when it rang a third time, he got up and began walking toward the living room until he heard his father severely demand, "Hello?" David froze just outside the living room where Pete had been sleeping in his recliner. David could see the muted television eerily flashing in the dark living room.

"What?" Pete demanded. "Who is this?" David remained silent and motionless, listening and holding his breath, ready to silently clear the hall should his mother or father get up and notice him eavesdropping.

"What do you want with David?" Pete demanded at last. At this, David's heart sank, pounding rapidly in his chest, and he was struggling to decide whether he should stroll in casually and take the phone or if he should scram and hide out in his room all day when Pete said, "I don't give a damn!" David immediately felt angry at his father for talking to Jess that way; Jess hadn't done anything wrong. He unconsciously decided to stroll in and take the phone before Pete could say more. "Don't you be fuckin' calling my phone this early in the goddamn morning—"

"Oh, is that Jess?" David asked. "He told me he was going to call this morning about a homework assignment," he lied.

Pete stared in disbelief, his mouth slightly agape, as it had frozen in mid-sentence. "You little shit," he muttered ominously as he hung up the phone, and though it wasn't clear whether he was talking to David or to Jess through the phone at that point, David flushed and became so miserably angry at his father that he could hold his tongue no longer.

"Hey, don't talk to Jess like that!"

Pete began struggling to hoist himself out of his recliner, and David's stomach squirmed at the acknowledgement of his outburst, but it had already gone too far. "Look, Jess didn't do anything wrong! He was just going to help me with homework."

"What the hell are you doing?" Janet's voice suddenly demanded from her bedroom door. David realized that she had just entered to see him yelling pleadingly at his father, who was still trying to get out of the chair. Her piercing tone startled David into a panic, and he immediately lunged forward and pushed Pete back down into the chair. Pete grunted in fury, and Janet shrieked again from the doorway and started toward David, but when David saw the rage in her eyes, which somehow made his father's contorted face look tame, he turned and ran to the back door. He slammed into it at full speed before tearing at the knob to unlock it and thrust it open. Then he swiftly slammed it shut, leapt over the short chain link fence surrounding their back yard, and ran all the way to Jess's house.

"Oh my gosh, I'm so sorry!" Jess exclaimed when he opened his front door for a panting, panicked David. "I had no idea—"

"No, it's fine," David interrupted, shaking his hands in the air. "You didn't do anything wrong. My parents are just crazy. I should have told you before." He gulped, now feeling vulnerable and very close to tears. This would be the first time he ever openly admitted to anyone that his parents were far less than desirable. "I was afraid you wouldn't want to hang out with me."

"Not want to hang out with you?" Jess seemed genuinely bewildered. "Come on, have you seen my parents at all this week? They're pretty much the same way. It's like they resent having to deal with me, so they almost never even speak to me. You can come here any time you need to, man. Seriously."

David struggled to catch his breath and to control the burning lump in his throat because of Jess's hospitality. He'd never had anyone offer him any understanding, and he'd certainly never been offered an escape, even if it was only a temporary one.

Jess walked out on the porch to sit on the stairs with David, and he was eventually able to set David's mind at ease. They talked for well over two hours about the comics David had recently finished. At about one o'clock, Jess offered to make them some sandwiches, and they continued chatting and laughing on the front porch while they ate in the bright midday sun.

By late afternoon David decided that he needed to get home and do some homework before bed, but as he was walking back home, he became feverish and trembly thinking about what his parents would do to him when they caught up with him next. He thought briefly of what Mr. Stewart and Jess had said about his house, but the overwhelming irrationality of it all was dwarfed by his insurmountable terror of what he'd done and what would inevitably be done to him as a result. He felt too nauseous to think as he turned onto Jade Street, and he knew that his only hope of getting through this was to avoid his parents for the rest of his life. The notion seemed completely plausible to David.

When he got to his house, he quietly went in the front door and crept straight to his bedroom. Then he just lay on his bed and stared at the ceiling, his mind strangely devoid of thought, looking at nothing, thinking nothing, until the room started spinning and blurring and tiny lights were flashing at the edges of his vision. Beginning to feel a little drowsy, not to mention worried about his bedroom door that wouldn't lock, he got some comic books and went outside to the front porch and sat reading in the warm sun. At least if he were accosted here, he had a viable escape route.

Three hours later he awoke, startled, and looked around. Finally, he realized where he was and calmed down a little. He had fallen asleep reading, and it had grown almost completely dark. Standing up and stretching, he gathered his books to go back inside, but something caught his eye from across the street. It was pretty dark out, and he couldn't tell what it was from so far away, so he started toward the street. Across the street was a telephone pole, and on it David noticed a sign. When he got closer to the pole, he could see that it read:

Shih Tzu
Free To Good Home
We can no longer care for our puppy. He is 3 weeks
old and has no name, a very friendly Shih Tzu, not yet
house-trained, and still feeds off a bottle.

There was a picture under this text, then:

For More Info. Call Megan Howell

It listed a number at the bottom. David pulled a pen from his pocket and copied it onto his hand as he considered the picture of the dog. *Where have I seen that dog? Isn't that Jess's? Wait, does Jess even have a dog?* He stared at the picture of the tiny puppy as his brain whirled. *I know that dog has something to do with Jess.* But he and Jess had been together only at school, on the bus, and at Jess's house. He must have seen the dog there. Then he remembered: *THE DREAM! That's it. Jess tripped in my dream, and his dog died.*

That wasn't quite right, but David began to feel uneasy. He felt as though he was being silly, but he could not shake the image of that dog. It was a tiny version of the shaggy dog that he had watched die in his dream. *But lots of dogs look the same. Stop trying to connect that picture with a weird dream you had weeks ago.* Slowly, he turned and went home, still pondering the profound déjà vu that he felt about the dog. He thought again of how strange the Stewarts and Jess had acted about his house, and he stopped in his driveway to stare at the building for nearly a full minute before he was able to shake the feeling. *Stop! You have bigger problems to deal with right now than some superstition or stupid dream.*

He gathered his books together and crept into the dark house through the front door, listening intently for any movement from his parents.

In his room he copied the phone number from his hand to a piece of paper and laid it on his desk and began to think of the dream again in spite of himself. Jess had fallen in the dream. His parents and the Stewarts were dead in the dream. He remembered that vividly. Then there was a girl, but who was that? He couldn't even envision her face now. And the garbage can. What was it about the garbage can? He remembered the feeling of adrenaline pumping through his body, forcing a sense of purpose into his brain. He remembered wanting to hurt someone. But who?

My God, David, it's just a dream. You're only chasing ghosts of random images from some stupid, meaningless dream.

But he wasn't chasing anything without reason.

His head swayed, and he soon fell asleep.

9

L ife went well for David for the next few weeks. His parents kept their
distance and never brought up the episode in the living room. Perhaps they thought that he had finally decided not to take their crap anymore. No one really tormented him at school. He and Jess remained fast
friends; they were extremely close, and at this point they knew almost
everything about each other (though Jess still hadn't come into David's
house). David never mentioned anything about the dream to Jess or anyone else. In fact, he had nearly forgotten it altogether. The sign on the
telephone pole had long since blown away, and David had completely
forgotten that he ever wrote down the number about the dog. He did not
have any recollection of ever writing the number at all.

Then, one weekend morning in late September, he was looking
out his bedroom window when he saw a girl with blonde hair putting
something on the telephone pole. When she turned and walked away, he
saw that it was a piece of paper, the same one about the dog. He guessed
that she was Megan, and he felt a little sorry for her, wondering why she
couldn't keep the dog for herself. He suddenly got a very uncharacteristic
desire to get up and run outside to talk to her, and by the time he realized
that this was absolutely insane, he was already rushing down the stairs to
try to catch up with her.

He burst out the front door and speed-walked across the street and
onto the sidewalk behind her. "Hey!" he called to get her to slow and turn
back, and when he finally caught up with her he saw that she was absolutely, indescribably beautiful. He almost screamed; his eyes widened,
and his mouth opened and just froze as his heart leapt into his throat and
paralyzed his vocal cords. He felt an even deeper sense of déjà vu than he
had felt when looking at the dog, but this was shadowed by his immense
fear of looking like an idiot. What had made this seem like a good idea
when he was watching from his window? Now that he was out here, he

had absolutely no idea what to say; her unadulterated beauty made him want to openly sob. He stood staring, thinking a thousand things at once, and a strange, strained grunt squeaked out of his open mouth.

"Hello?" the girl finally asked, obviously unnerved by David's strange appearance.

David nearly threw up on the spot. "Um . . . sorry." He hurried past her, and, realizing how ridiculous he must look, he added, "I thought you were someone else." He tried to justify his awkwardness, but his timing only made him seem stranger.

He walked quickly enough to outpace the girl, and he continued on around the corner, heading nowhere, to avoid letting her see him walk back into his house like a complete moron. Maybe his sense of purpose could serve to distract her from the ridiculousness of his greeting. He kept glancing back over his shoulder to see where she was going, and when she continued walking around the block to put up more signs, he hurried around the block in the opposite direction in order to loop back to his house.

He started thinking back on his dream from several weeks ago. At this point it was just too overwhelming to continue denying that he had dreamt of all these people who were coming into his life, but he had no idea what any of it could mean. He wondered if it was a sign that his parents were dying, and his skin flushed and got hot and feverish all over, but he couldn't quite decide whether or not this was a bad thing. Then he remembered the gorgeous girl in his dream walking away from him and joining some group of people, and his baser instinct to secure her as his own hit him like a strange jolt of electricity. What chance did he have of "securing" a girl like that? But still, in the dream she had walked away from him when he wouldn't acknowledge her.

"Oh, stop!" he suddenly yelled at the quiet neighborhood. His heart was beating fast, and he suddenly had to pee. "It was a stupid dream. Weeks ago!" He was angry with himself for being so preoccupied with something so ridiculous, but when he reached his house again, he stopped by the garbage can and studied his house. It was hard to deny how quickly his will to talk to the girl had faded once he left the house; he wondered if he might be able to use its power—the house's power—to his advantage. Of course, it was ridiculous to think that a house had powers or gave power to its inhabitants, but he had stood up to his parents twice now, seemingly gotten them off his back, and gotten the courage to talk to Jess since he had moved in. Maybe it wouldn't hurt to give the girl a call from inside the house, where he wouldn't be so vulnerable.

"I can't believe I'm even considering this," he muttered to himself before heading inside, but as soon as he walked through the door, he definitely felt suddenly more composed and ready to call the number from the sign. He no longer even considered how creepy he would seem if or when the girl found out that he was the one calling her.

He snuck the telephone off the receiver in the empty living room and quietly headed upstairs to find the paper where he'd written the phone number.

As the phone was ringing, a sickening knot curled in his gut, but he swallowed hard and convinced himself that inside this house he was going to do fine, inside this house he had confidence. Still, he had a compelling urge to drop the phone and rush to the bathroom.

"Hello?" a familiar voice said just as he was beginning to wonder if he'd given her enough time to finish putting up the new signs.

"Uh . . . um, is this Megan?" he asked, dumbly clearing his throat.

"Yes," she replied slowly, sounding confused now.

"Um, I'm . . . " he paused far too long, "David." He sounded even more dumb now, and the house did not seem to be affording him any assistance. She must think he had been fumbling to make a name up on the spot for whatever reason. "I . . . " he paused again, realizing that he had no idea why he had wanted to call in the first place. "I'll take your dog. I was going to call last time the sign was up, but I never got around to it."

"Oh, ok," she said less slowly, sounding hopeful now. David wondered again how he could have been so stupid as to run outside to greet a strange girl. Exactly from where had that cataclysmic courage come? And now he had been even more stupid to call that same girl with absolutely nothing to say, and he had screwed it up worse by being a coward and blatantly changing the topic of interest from her to her dog. Now he would be obligated to actually take her dog, especially if he ever wanted to talk to her again. He knew that he had never really intended to call when he wrote that number down weeks ago. In fact, he had no idea why he had saved the phone number in the first place.

"Sorry, um . . . we just moved in a few months ago . . . in August, I think." He was remembering how attractive she had been on the sidewalk, and he was desperately trying to redeem his rocky start with her. An unfamiliar warmth spread like a shiver from his lower abdomen down his legs. She had a nice voice too, and he had no idea what he was saying out loud anymore.

"All right," she said, sounding confused again. "You can come to my house and get him whenever you'd like." Business as usual.

"Uh, okay." David's stomach tightened again, and he wanted to puke as he tried to think of anything to talk about besides her dog. Megan gave him her address, and he wrote down the house number. When she hung up, he sat there in a dry-mouthed silence with the phone still pressed tightly to his ear until he heard the screeching tone in his ear that told him the other line was disconnected.

Now he was either going to have to give up on talking to this girl—who may not even be interested in talking to *him*—or he'd have to walk over to her house and take her stupid dog.

He threw the phone at the ground near the door. Though he was careful not to throw it directly at the wall, lest it cause damage or make noise, he was shocked by his outburst, so he closed his eyes and tried to calm down.

Maybe this would be okay. Maybe he'd think of something better to say when he got there.

That's ridiculous. You're going to freeze up like you always do. You couldn't even pull this off in the house, over the phone!

He groaned in aggravation and got up to retrieve the phone, whose back plate had flown across the room when it hit the door.

Ultimately David's nature left him feeling obligated to take the little dog off Megan's hands after getting her hopes up with the atrocious phone call. He decided that going over to her house and talking to her might not be the worst thing in the world. Yes, she was a beautiful girl, but he had managed to maintain conversation with Jess, and maybe he could pull it off again with Megan.

Before leaving he changed his shirt with the naive hope that Megan wouldn't recognize him from mere minutes before. He walked out of the house and around the corner then began checking mailboxes for her house number. When he finally found her house about two blocks past the corner, his mouth was dry, and his stomach was doing somersaults, but he continued walking toward her front porch as his vision swayed with every pound of his heart against his chest.

Megan answered the door almost immediately and was already holding the small puppy in her arms. At first she looked surprised to see

David again, but she seemed to accept it and said, "Oh, are you David?"

"Yeah," he said, grinning moronically.

She smiled kindly and asked, "Didn't I just see you when I was putting signs up?"

David's stomach lurched. Now she knew he had been stalking her before he called her like a pathetic, incompetent jerk. "Oh, um, yeah. I was out, and I noticed the signs again," he lied, "Thought I'd give you a call." Luckily she didn't press him further.

She just smiled even more remarkably and said, "Well, this is Shaggy." She held out the puppy for David to take, but he stood there reluctantly. "You can hold him. It's fine. You have to see if you get along." She giggled adorably, and David reached out to take Shaggy from her. His skin tingled all over as his hand brushed hers in the exchange. "No one came to get him a month ago when I put the signs out, so I had to give him a name while he was still young enough to learn it."

"It's a good name," was all David could think to say. The dog was shaggy after all. He was so small; he fit into David's cupped palms, and he licked David's arm sleepily. Suddenly David felt very glad he had agreed to take the dog anyway. His parents would never go for it, obviously, but maybe he could work something out. He would worry about that when the time came. If nothing else, he could give it to Jess or take it to an animal shelter. This thought filled him with a new pang of helpless guilt. What would she think of someone who would take this dog from her and immediately turn it over to an overpopulated shelter that would destroy it in a matter of weeks?

"Yeah, he's also house-trained now, and he started eating dry food recently." She looked as though she would cry, and David realized that she didn't want to lose the dog; she must have had no choice. "I begged my parents not to take him to the shelter, but they said that another week was all they'd give me. Thank you so much for taking him. Please take good care of him."

Great, now it was all on him. He looked into her gleaming eyes and thought that he would do just about anything within his power to avoid ever seeing them shed a tear of sadness. Come hell or high waters, there would be no animal shelters in Shaggy's future.

"Oh, I will. Don't worry." He paused, suddenly inspired and excited by a perfect idea. "You know, if you want to come see him sometime, feel free." His heart was pounding in his chest as he waited to see how she would react to this quasi-invitation.

She smiled again immediately. It was such a pretty smile. "I'd like that."

At that, David smiled too. "I live just around the corner down there." He pointed down the road to Jade Street and held Shaggy to his chest with one arm.

"I noticed that," she said, smiling coyly. "It looked like you're staying in the Batterman house." She said the name in a sarcastically ominous tone.

"Oh, yeah." David looked down at his shoes, feeling almost guilty despite the fact that Megan was grinning.

She obviously noticed his expression, because she became more serious. "Oh, I just heard it was—"

He cut her off, "Yeah, yeah, I know." Now his chance to hang out with a beautiful girl was shot because of his stupid house.

"Oh, I'm sorry. I was only kidding. That's just some dumb story that kids made up. I mean," she paused, "Mr. Batterman may have really had issues, but that doesn't affect the value of the real-estate." She smirked again, apparently more entertained with her playfulness than David was at that moment.

"No, it's okay. I know that. It's just that no one else seems to."

"Well, people can be childish, especially when everyone else around them is being even more childish. It makes it easier." She smiled kindly at David again and touched his arm, which was holding the tiny sleeping dog. His body tingled again, and his stomach rolled as his heart sped up even more. He looked into her piercing, calming blue eyes and was startled to find himself thinking plainly, *she's even better than in the dream.*

"You can come in if you'd still like to take him. There's no reason to keep standing out here with the door open," she said. They stepped inside together and she told David that he could put Shaggy down and let him run around. "So what do you think?"

Now that he had come this far, taking the dog to a shelter was no longer an option; he couldn't be responsible for doing that to Megan. He would either have to hide the dog away in his house or convince his parents to allow him to keep him. He smiled, nonetheless, "I'll keep him."

Megan was practically beaming now. "Great! I still have a little food for him I can give you, and he has a couple toys that I got him. Plus a bed and some old blankets that I'll let him keep."

"Oh, wow," David said, "That's great." But he realized that he had no way to get money for food for the dog. Even if, by some miracle, his parents allowed him to keep the dog, they would never agree to buy food for him.

Megan continued smiling and thanking David, and while David wasn't brave enough to give her his phone number, he suggested that she just stop by and knock on his door outside of school hours whenever she wanted to visit Shaggy. He imagined that she would never actually show up and that she would forget all about Shaggy in a matter of days, so he didn't really worry about her running into his parents.

After they bid their awkward farewells, David walked home with a sack full of doggy provisions in one hand and a sleepy puppy in the other. Though pleased by this initial encounter, he felt exceptionally downhearted as he left her house. He doubted if she would ever show him as much attention in the future and wondered how in the world he had ended up with this poor dog that he'd never be able to keep.

When he got back to his house, David decided that the safest course of action for the time being would be to just take the dog to his room and try to hide it away from his parents. He would lock Shaggy in his bedroom while he was at school and feed and walk him every day immediately after. His parents would probably never notice. David had the entire upstairs to himself; they rarely went upstairs, and they never went into his room.

He closed his bedroom door and set Shaggy on the ground to investigate, willing him not to bark or make any noise. He set Shaggy's bed and food bowl in the corner, along with a couple toys that didn't squeak, and got into his bed to read for a while. After a few minutes, though, Shaggy started whining and grumbling quietly at the side of David's bed, pawing his dangling comforter. David smiled and leaned over to pick up the dog and let it get on the bed. Shaggy nuzzled at David's side for a bit, licked his arm, and finally curled up to sleep in the warmth of David's armpit. As David let his book rest more and more on his stomach and finally closed his eyes to drift into an early afternoon nap, he felt kind of glad that he had taken the dog after all. He scratched Shaggy's head as they both fell asleep, and he found comfort just in having the company.

10

Monday morning David got Shaggy settled into his little bed and pleaded quietly with him not to get restless or whiny during the day. God only knew what his parents would do if they heard a dog barking.

When the bus arrived at his house that afternoon, he immediately rushed inside and ran upstairs to check on Shaggy. He saw that he had gone to the bathroom on his floor twice while he was in school, but he didn't get angry; he just sighed. "Come on, buddy," David squatted to pat Shaggy's head because he seemed to detect the disappointment in his new owner's voice; his ears and tail drooped, and his eyes dropped to the floor. "I know it's hard being stuck in here all day, but there's no other way." He stood up and went to the kitchen to get some cleaning products and paper towels then returned to his room to let Shaggy watch him clean up the mess.

"Come on out," he said when he finished cleaning, patting his leg. "I'll take you out every day when I get home, but you have to try to be good while I'm gone."

Shaggy stood and slowly came to David's feet and allowed himself to be picked up. David made sure that his parents weren't in the kitchen or hallway and made his way outside, Shaggy in one hand and Jess's latest stack of comic books in the other. He put Shaggy down in the grass and started walking toward Jess's house, allowing Shaggy to simultaneously explore and learn to follow him while they walked. David was excited to show Jess his new pet. He hadn't given away the surprise at school, only the fact that there was a surprise.

When Shaggy found a spot in the grass to do his business again, David made a point in congratulating and patting him profusely, hoping that this positive reinforcement would help him learn what was right. In fact, Shaggy made a small mess on David's floor Tuesday, and by

Wednesday he had learned the routine; he never had another accident.

Jess was excited for David when he met Shaggy, and Shaggy seemed just as excited to meet Jess, if not more so. Jess didn't bother asking any uncomfortable questions about how David was managing to keep the little guy in his house with his parents. That was one of the great things about Jess. He didn't have to know every excruciating detail, and he somehow knew which details were okay to investigate.

Shaggy fell into the daily routine quite readily: wait for David to return from school, follow David outside, do his business, follow David to Jess's house, play fetch and roll around in Jess's yard and on his porch, follow David home and do his business one last time, then go inside and get cozy for bed. He somehow knew better than to rush downstairs and investigate the house; he stood each day at David's open bedroom door waiting for a signal from David to hop into his arms and be charioted downstairs and out the front door. David imagined that his parents must be giving off some pretty foul pheromones to repel even something as curious as a young dog, and he was profoundly grateful to have been graced with such an easy-going, well-trained companion.

On Wednesday David and Jess were making plans to watch the second Superman movie that weekend while Shaggy dragged his raggedy stuffed ostrich through Jess's yard. He'd bring it back to one of the two boys to throw it again and again, never tiring. On the way back from Jess's house, David saw the brilliant shine of the evening sunlight on Megan's immaculate blonde hair. She was walking toward the two of them on the other side of the street before she stopped at the streetlight; David saw she was taking down her signs.

"Hey!" he called from less than a block away as he waved one hand above his head and quickened his pace to meet her.

"Oh, hey there," she said, beaming, when he and Shaggy reached her. "I was just thinking about stopping by today."

David was kind of taken aback. "Really? I didn't . . ." he trailed off.

She must have seen the confusion on his face. "I told you I'd like to come by. I just wanted to check and see how Shaggy was doing," she justified hastily.

"Oh, no. I remember. I just didn't think you actually would," David said reluctantly.

Megan smiled anew and bent to receive Shaggy, who was nearly doing backflips at her feet. "Well I meant it. Of course I would. How could I not want to visit this little guy?" She glanced up coyly at David, and his skin seemed to tighten all over his body. He chuckled dryly, feeling extraordinarily awkward and unworthy in the presence of a goddess.

"Is something wrong?" she asked, standing up with Shaggy. Her lusty playfulness transitioned to concern so smoothly that David's head swam, and he actually had to convince himself not to seize her face and deliver what would likely be the most disappointing and awkward kiss of her life.

He swallowed hard and tried to remain calm and keep a friendly smile on his face. "Oh, no. I'm good."

She grinned cutely and dropped her gaze minutely only to look back up at David and say, "You're all flustered." David had an idea that she had consciously acted more awkward and shy to make him feel less uncomfortable, and he was amazed to find that it had worked. He actually laughed normally.

"Sorry. You're just . . . " he paused indefinitely, desperately trying to think of a good word to describe her. "I don't know . . . funny." It was a terrible word, and it was definitely a terrible word to describe this girl with whom he was inescapably infatuated, but she seemed understanding and flattered nonetheless.

The ensuing silence was strangely comforting to David, and it lasted the ideal amount of time before she made a perfect transition to casual conversation. "So how has he been?"

"Oh, he's great. Really, I couldn't ask for a better dog."

"That's great!" she seemed as genuinely happy for David as he knew she was for Shaggy. "I can't thank you enough for giving him a good home. I thought we'd never get rid of him." She laughed a little and pointed to the pole where her sign had just been hanging. "Of course I've had two calls since you came and got him, so I figured I'd better come take these down."

"Well, I'm glad you did," David said automatically. Her eyes shot back to his in obvious surprise, and he quickly said, "I mean, I'm glad I met you here." That wasn't quite right. "I mean, I'm glad I met you in time to get him first. He's great."

Megan chuckled loudly, obviously entertained by David's stammering, and David could almost feel his body being physically drawn to her tiny, perfect, undetectable gravitational field. "So, you're in high school around here, right?" he asked.

"Yep. Tenth grade at Windsor Academy just outside the city. I'm guessing you're in Thriftson County High?"

"Oh, yeah. So how is private school?"

She grunted in disgust. "It's fantastic. Our advances in education far outweigh the social incompetency of the tools I am forced to mingle with."

"Um—" David stammered again.

"I'm just being sarcastic," she said. "It's awful. From what I know, our curriculum isn't really any different from yours, the teachers are hardly more qualified than yours, and my classmates are all total morons."

"Wow," David said, taken aback by her flawless ability to be adorable even while being sarcastic and biting. "Don't feel too bad. My classmates are morons, too."

"Well at least you all know how to talk to girls. It's high school for God's sake!"

"But," David laughed dryly again, "I don't know how to talk to girls." Megan's candidness and easygoing nature were giving him the confidence to open up a little and speak freely with her.

"You seem better at it than anyone at my school!" Megan replied.

David blushed but laughed with a little more humor. "Well, you must be like a queen at your school, then, but I probably belong with your classmates."

"Oh, you're cute. Don't be so hard on yourself," she said as she reached out and touched his wrist.

David's smile widened despite the fact that he felt as though his heart would force so much blood into his face that his eyes would pop out of their sockets. "You wouldn't happen to know Jess Stevens, would you?" he asked.

"No, why?"

"Oh, I don't know," David replied, smile faltering, desperate not to give Megan the wrong impression of himself. "He lives in this neighborhood too. He's pretty much my only friend from school."

"Oh." She finally seemed at a loss for something to say, but then she smiled again, same as ever. "Well, then you're all set. Two friends in the same neighborhood. Who needs anyone else from school?"

She was absolutely a breath of fresh air in David's stale, recycled, polluted atmosphere. He had thought that Jess was as good as it got, but

Megan made him feel so at ease that he could talk about almost anything.

But one problem still remained. He had absolutely no way to get food for Shaggy, and to admit this to Megan might show her what a loser David really was. He had been growing more and more concerned each day as Shaggy's bag of food dwindled, and he'd already explored every option. He would rather open up to any other person on the planet about this problem, but he felt that Megan would be the one most likely to care enough to help him. He'd have to tell her, even if that meant opening her eyes to David's unfavorable situation.

"Listen, I . . . " he could think of no way to even begin, could think of no good way to embark on a necessary conversation that may promptly close the book on this exciting new chapter in his life. "I don't . . . my family situation is . . . it's just that my parents aren't really a big help with Shaggy." He paused again, hoping that she would fill in the blanks, but Megan only stared expressionlessly. "I don't have any way to feed him," he finished bluntly.

Blessedly, her lovely smile returned, and she said, "Are you asking me to feed your dog, David?" Her tone was amiable enough, but David felt sick and ashamed.

"I just wanted you to know. I don't want something bad to happen that I can't control . . ."

She seemed unconcerned. "Well my father's lab eats dog food that isn't too terribly large," she sighed theatrically, but her smile showed that she was yet again pulling David's leg. "I suppose I could steal some from him and bring it to you sometimes."

Of all the infinite possibilities of responses that she could have given, this would have been the one David would have bet against, but he was quickly finding that Megan tended to be almost everything pleasant that one would least expect in an individual. He smiled back now, looking up from his shoes. "I guess that means we'll have to see each other more often, then."

David laughed aloud at his unexpected smoothness, and Megan joined in, something that David, whose self worth had been unhealthily low for years, could barely comprehend.

The two talked for nearly thirty more minutes, just standing in the sidewalk, and when the streetlight flickered on above them, they simultaneously seemed to snap out of their trance of mutual infatuation. Megan said, "Well, I guess I'd better be getting home." She pet Shaggy, who was now sleeping in the grass between her legs, one last time and stood up with David. He told her that every day after school he and Shaggy walked to Jess's house around the corner and that he would love for her to join up with them whenever she had time.

As they were making their final goodbyes, Megan surprised David one last time by pulling him close to her and giving him an enthusiastic hug. He took in every second of her warmth and his hands on her smooth arms, and when they finally pulled apart, he realized that he hadn't been breathing. He suddenly gasped in a breath of air and blushed when he realized how obvious it was to Megan, but she just giggled in her adorable way and bit her lower lip as she turned away and started walking home.

David stood where he was for a bit, overwhelmed with emotion. He had a new friend, a new dog, and a girl who actually paid attention to him, all in barely more than a month, and he couldn't remember ever being so happy in his life.

Lying in bed that night, he had unfamiliar fantasies of feeling Megan's firm body against his in embrace, and he woke up twice in the night sweating and dry-mouthed after dreaming about kissing her in outlandishly fantastic venues and fashions.

Megan and Jess met the next day, and her existence gave David and Jess something new to talk about while she wasn't around. The three of them never ventured into David's house; they just sat at the curb or on Jess's front porch and played with Shaggy and talked and joked. Megan was surprisingly interested in Jess's comic books and movies, but David was discovering that he shouldn't bother being surprised by the growing list of her innumerable perfections. He never asked Megan why she hadn't been able to keep Shaggy, but he didn't think he needed to. He had a feeling that the three of them became so close due partly to their all being in similar domestic situations. He quickly grew to care for both of them immensely, and he would have done anything for them.

11

David and Megan were sitting on the curb across the street from his house on Friday evening. The afternoon was growing dark, and Jess had just gone home, leaving David to reflect on how grateful he felt toward Megan and how he didn't really understand the status of their relationship. He didn't really know much about her life away from the curb on Jade Street, and he wanted to find out. He wanted to claim her as his own and find out everything about her and express the gratitude he felt at having her as a friend. Not to mention the fact that he found himself more and more unable to escape the tantalizing thoughts and dreams that he was having about her, and no matter how open and friendly she acted toward him, he just couldn't convince himself that she felt anywhere near the same way as he did.

"You and Jess and Shaggy are the only real friends I've ever had," he said abruptly, unable to think of anything to say that wouldn't sound dumb. "I don't know what I would do without you." Megan smiled, and when he saw it, he decided that he didn't care anymore about how dumb he sounded.

But just then he noticed his mother storming out of the front door and glaring at the two of them.

"Oh man!" he whispered, "I have to go. I'm sorry. Take Shaggy. I'll call you later."

"Okay, bye!" Megan hastily squeezed David's hand, scooped up the sleeping Shaggy, and got up to walk swiftly home.

"David Slate, what are you doing with a filthy little girl?" Janet bellowed across the street as David stood and started toward the house.

He had suddenly gone from being almost euphoric with love to being scared out of his mind. "Nothing, mom. Please!" Then he saw the look of absolute murder in her eyes and felt even worse. "Oh, God."

David reached her at the end of his driveway with his arms

stretched out in a pleading gesture. Janet grabbed his hair and whipped his head toward her body as she did an about-face and started back toward the front door.

"Oh, no. We're going to see your father and we'll all talk about it together!" She continued screeching like a harpy, obviously trying to melt David's brain, despite the fact that he was now being dragged along right at her side. All he could do now was hope that Megan was still going the other way and not watching the outrageous spectacle that Janet was making.

"PETE!" she barked into the front door, which she had left standing open.

She wasn't even bothering to feign good nature or caustic sweetness, and this really terrified David; he was on the verge of tears from humiliation and fear. Why couldn't his mother just continue to ignore him? It was as though she sometimes wanted to pick fights. He could think of no indication that she cared at all about what he did or with whom he did it. He was just a resilient pet on whom she and Pete could take out their aggravation.

David imagined Megan watching from behind a tree as they started up the porch steps, Janet dragging him by his hair.

"Oh, Petie!" Janet adopted her sickly sarcastic voice once they had reached the door and got it closed behind them. "Your son is screwing around with some trashy girl!" At this, David's fear left, and he was suddenly filled with anger and confidence. Janet was just putting on a show to humiliate him.

"She is not trashy," he said, rage building, as he slapped his mother's hand out of his hair and stood upright. "She is very kind, and she's one of my few friends . . . and we weren't screwing around," he added.

Janet looked a little taken aback at David's outburst, but she ignored him and turned toward the approaching sounds of Pete's heavy footsteps. She proclaimed to anyone who was listening, "*We* will not be responsible for taking care of any bastard grandchildren!"

Then Pete entered, looking almost as mad as David now felt, but there was an obvious expression of eager excitement on his face, just like a man going into a huge, season-ending sporting event. Pete was ready to harass David simply for the thrill.

"You're just mad because I have some friends now and am not miserable in here with you all day."

"You are not going to talk to us like that, young man." Pete said, advancing on him menacingly. David was appalled by the transition and difference between almost-comatose Pete and ready-to-tango Pete.

"I'll talk to you how I want. You never think about how you talk to me!" David yelled back confidently.

Pete raised his hand to slap David. "What did you say?" he demanded.

"You heard me." David stood his ground, not concerned in the slightest about outcomes at this point. "Or is all of that booze clouding your ears as well your brain?"

Janet gasped, and David did too, for his father's hand had come down so hard across his face that he fell to the ground and slid across the kitchen floor a few feet. A red haze filled David's field of vision, but he was in too much pain to lash out at his father. He moaned aloud because it was the only way that he felt able to convey his irritation. Oddly enough, he felt more irritated than anything. He felt annoyed that his father was enjoying this abuse without cause, and because he couldn't return the favor to his overweight excuse for a dad. David wanted nothing more than to leap from the ground and return his father's sadistic beatings. He didn't even care if he lost, if he wound up dead; he just wanted to fight back for once. He caught a trace of how his father must feel: his heart was racing from something resembling excitement, and he wanted to fight simply for the thrill of the fight, not for victory and not to set an example.

But his adrenaline-soaked organs turned to quickly pulsing filters for fear when Pete grabbed his ankles and pulled him toward himself. When he was able to reach his collar, Pete lifted David's body from the floor and pushed it into the wall. David felt his head smash a dent into the drywall, and his father reached into the kitchen sink to grab a thick-bristled scrubbing brush almost like one used to clean a toilet. He backed up and released David, leaving him standing numbly and wavering against the wall, and cocked back his arm to swing the brush at his son. David saw through swelling eyes the ridiculously fat, bald man before him swinging a brush that was tiny in comparison to his meaty fist, and he almost laughed at the comical sight. But when the brush connected with his cheek, he felt the sharp bristles carve lines in his flesh, drawing blood instantly, and he felt the hard handle connect with bone and push his jaw too far to the right, whipping his head and neck violently to the side. He fell to the floor and tried to stay on his stomach.

"Hey, hey! Mister Ninth-Grade-Know-It-All's gonna lose that bitter tongue!" Pete called tauntingly like a high-school bully. He kicked David's ribs and turned him over. "You didn't bite it off, did ya? Thought I saw some blood before you even hit the ground!" David saw the glee on his father's face as he swung the brush down again and again and again, hitting him more with his balled fist than with the plastic brush, until everything went black.

———————————

He awoke in his bedroom floor the next morning. Looking around and gathering himself, he wondered how his parents had dragged his limp body all the way in here and not noticed the bowl of dog food in the corner, next to a tiny bed. Or maybe they had noticed and had taken their anger out on his already unconscious figure, and that could be the end of it.

His head hurt so terribly that he could barely move his hands without his throbbing neurons flaring up in protesting pain, but he immediately made his way downstairs to call Megan. He didn't tell her what happened for the same reason he never told anyone about his parents' behavior: he was afraid of what might happen and of what people might think of him. But he knew that Megan knew.

"Hello?" her beautiful voice asked, interrupting his thoughts.

"Hey, it's David." He was talking quietly in case his parents were awake, but he was desperate to finish what he had started yesterday. He hated his mother for choosing that moment to interrupt them that way.

"How are you?" she sounded so concerned, almost like she might have just finished crying.

"Oh, I'm okay," he lied. His head was still sore from the row, and he felt slightly nauseous. Although the slashes in his cheek stung bitterly and bled thin, bright-red plasma, they were shallow, and he would be able to pass them off as the result of a scrape from asphalt until they were gone, and the bruise on his jaw hadn't become too pronounced.

"I'm so sorry, David. I didn't mean to get you into trouble—"

He cut her off. "You didn't do anything wrong. She doesn't even care what I do. I guess she just needed a punching bag last night."

"Oh, David. Are you sure you're all right?"

"Yeah, fine. I can't really talk long, but I just wanted to apologize for the way we were cut off yesterday." At this point, David didn't care how awkward or dumb he sounded. He was trying to do this last night, and his mother had ruined it completely. Plus, this was markedly less awkward over the phone.

"You're so sweet," she said, sounding somewhat normal again. He could tell that she was smiling.

"I care a lot about you," he explained, "and I was just wondering . . ." Suddenly he had no idea what he planned to say. "Um . . . err . . . " He was freezing up, even over the phone. Maybe it was a good thing he had been interrupted last night. Otherwise he would have looked this foolish in person.

Then she made it worse by interjecting, "What is it, David?" She sounded genuinely curious.

He had to make a conscious decision to force himself to keep going, just as though he were forcing himself to dive into a pool of water that he knew was painfully cold. "Would you ever . . ." What? Ever what? "Ever go out with me?" What did that even mean? They had been "out" a hundred times.

But Megan obviously knew what he was getting at. "Oh, of course!" she exclaimed immediately, as if she knew where he was headed all along. "I've been waiting so long for you to ask."

David's stomach turned from painfully nauseous to delightfully billowy in a mere nanosecond. His body tingled in the now-familiar way, and he was shocked and excited that she had actually been waiting for this from him. He had absolutely nothing to say, could do nothing but grin foolishly in his empty room with the phone pressed against his ear.

Megan giggled into the silence, and now David wished with all his heart that he had been able to do this in person. Of course, he had never kissed a girl, but he felt that this could have been a perfect first time, and here he was stuck in his stupid room with a throbbing head and stinging cheek. Not even Shaggy was around to celebrate with him.

"Oh, how is Shaggy?" He finally remembered that she had taken him with her when Janet stormed out. "I hope it wasn't a problem having him stay with you last night."

"No, not at all. He's fine. You can get him whenever you like."

They talked for a few more minutes about Shaggy, and David was relieved at the convenient change of subject to break their silence, but he did wish that he could go back to that silence for a bit. Actually, he wished he could enjoy that silence alone with Megan, perhaps with her hand in his own, or even with her tongue in his mouth. He wished that his feelings of excitement and happiness and his desire to touch Megan's perfect skin didn't have to be associated with the nauseous shame in his gut that his parents had instilled.

12

Later Saturday evening, after David had finished his homework, he walked downstairs to browse the kitchen. He noticed that his mother was away, and when he saw his father punishing the chair with his girth, he grinned sadistically.

"Get me a beer," Pete called when David walked into the kitchen, and before realizing it, David had chuckled out loud.

"Oh," Pete muttered upon realizing that it was David in the kitchen and not Janet. "What's so bloomin' funny?" he yelled, sounding irate.

David's newfound quick tongue got the better of him. "It's just that your walrus body doesn't match the childish innocence that you claim by assuming I owe you any favors." He heard his father getting out of the chair.

"Where in the wide, wide world did you come about such a smart mouth?" he demanded.

"I guess I'm just finally starting to realize how pathetic you really are," David returned. "I don't owe you anything, and I'll do my best to make sure that you have a terribly hard time indulging yourself with more irresponsible behaviors. Believe it or not, they actually make you harder to tolerate." He walked to the refrigerator, took out a bottle of his father's alcohol, and smashed it all over the edge of the counter, thinking nothing except how desperately he hated this man for everything he had done, for everything he was. The notion had been within David for years, but today it seemed to have novel clarity in his mind.

Pete stood, surprisingly calm, while David, in his own mind, was panicking. He was filled with hatred and rage and wanted nothing more than to plunge both his thumbs into his father's eye sockets, but his mind was screaming to stop, screaming that he was losing control and fighting a losing battle with a monster. David's body wanted to fight, regardless. An onlooker would never have known of this turmoil going on in his brain; David showed no outward signs of discomfort or unrest. He simply glared.

Pete moved toward David with a wicked grin forming at the edges of his mouth. "You owe me your life. You owe me and your mom everything. You wouldn't be here if not for us."

"Then there's one more thing I can hold against you! I despise you for bringing me into this home, and I wish every day that it could have been any other two people on the planet!" David barked, beginning to breathe heavily, his chest finally heaving and displaying his agitation.

"You think you're growing up mighty fast, little man, and it's going to get you into a world of trouble. You think that you're better than us. You think you finally understand your life, but I have news for you . . ." Pete quickly hauled David up by the neck before he could react and pressed his back against the freezer. He was smiling, but David no longer felt the urge to fight merely for the fight. He was no longer filled with belligerent excitement; he was overcome with a simple desire to kill his father on the spot. He knew that he could if he tried. Would Pete ever expect that? He suddenly wondered why his parents had never actually killed him.

David began flailing about, grabbing and scratching at his father's arms that were wrapped around his neck, blocking his airway. He snatched behind his back at the door of the refrigerator and popped it open. It didn't help anything at all; Pete's grip held firm. Pete pushed David aside, reached into the open refrigerator, pulled out another bottle, and hit David directly in the side of the head with it, hard enough to still David's flailing but not quite hard enough to break the bottle. David thought wildly that Pete simply couldn't bear to waste another few ounces. Pete dropped him on the floor and began walking back to his chair with the bottle still in his hand. David squinted his eyes against the pain and called, "What's the matter? Is that all you've got? Why won't you just finish the job for once? I mean, I'm still conscious. Oh, I get it. Mom's not here, so you have no reason to display your caveman strength, right?"

Pete turned back around, looking more annoyed than shocked at his son's taunts and outbursts. It seemed that he had already come to expect things like this from David now. "You want it, you got it," he said plainly, walking toward the boy, still on his hands and knees on the floor.

When he was close enough, David quickly jerked a long piece of jagged plastic from the base of the refrigerator and, in one fluid motion, stood and swung it into Pete's face, producing a satisfying crack. In his surprise, Pete dropped his bottle and grasped at his stinging cheek. David grabbed the fallen bottle and swung with superhuman strength at his father's chunky shoulder. The bottle didn't break; it rebounded from Pete's shoulder blade and slipped from David's hand, the sharp cap cutting his palm. David was frantic, snatching things off the countertops, opening drawers, and throwing things: spoons, forks, knives, cups, can openers, whisks. He eventually got to the heavier pots and pans near the floor. The clamor was deafening. He ripped the toaster oven from the wall and hurled it across the kitchen, striking Pete's flailing forearm and making him howl with surprise. He yanked the metal guards from every burner on the stove and spun them through the air like deadly Frisbees, delivering bruises and cuts on Pete's arms, chest, and stomach. Swears and shrieks of rage from both Pete and David filled the room, accompanied by the clash of metal and plastic slamming into flesh and bone and linoleum and drywall.

Pete made his way toward David, batting away the flying objects. David thrust himself at his father and began battering his head with items of all sizes. Pete ducked, screaming and trying to protect himself.

Finally, David leapt onto the counter with a large knife in his hand and stopped his attack. "Try me again. I swear I'll kill you!"

At this, new rage seemed to flare inside of Pete. He raced around the corner and tore a banister from the stairwell. Fear returned when David saw his father come toward him with the wooden stake, sharp and jagged on both ends, and he immediately regretted his hasty death-threat. He frantically looked for anything bigger than the knife to defend himself. Pete swung the makeshift bat at his shins, splintering the wood with a grand-slam crack. David came down hard on his knees, and Pete grabbed his sweaty shirt and forcefully flung his body from the counter to the floor, whirling David's limp, surprised body around to land on its back. As if the contact with the floor wasn't enough to render David unconscious, his father brought the stub of wood down on the side of his turned head, and David felt no more until he awoke on his bedroom floor the next day.

13

That day David did nothing but sleep. When he awoke Monday morning to find his head still throbbing and his shins still dark purple and too painful to walk on, he decided not to go to school and to just sleep the day away again.

He finally returned to school on Wednesday. His hair covered most of his worst wounds, and his clothes covered the rest, so he knew that he could avoid any awkward questions. He had scarcely eaten since the previous Friday, and he thought that he had noticeably lost a bit of weight, but with his clothes, he thought that no one should notice.

Once on the bus, however, Jess voiced concern about his absences more than his appearance. David shut him up by saying that he had had a fever all weekend and just wanted to sleep it off, but Jess was still inquisitive, claiming that David seemed a little on-edge. David assured Jess that he shouldn't worry and that he was still very much looking forward to hanging out that afternoon.

At lunch that day, Jess watched David devour the sub-par cafeteria meal with an openly concerned look on his face. "Are you sure you're all right?"

"I'm fine," David maintained with irritation. Couldn't Jess tell that he had nothing that he wanted to discuss?

"It's just that you're eating really fast, and you seem kind of distracted."

David rolled his eyes. "I didn't have anything good to eat this weekend, so I'm hungry, all right? God, I don't see why you're getting so worked up because I'm eating more than normal."

"Okay, I'm sorry," Jess said timidly.

After lunch they walked to their lockers in strained silence, and when David saw the pack of upperclassmen, now led by an even older senior by the name of Justin Guy, he knew that he was not going to make it through this day.

Please, just shut up for one day, David thought. *Just one day without harassment is not too much to ask.*

"Well here's our cutest couple now!" the usual junior jock exclaimed loudly.

David wasted no time trying to maintain his already shaky composure. "Will you just shut up for once?" he snapped.

Everyone in the group laughed uproariously. They all loved when they got a reaction. "What is it?" Justin butted in sarcastically. "We just wanted to tell y'all they need you for pictures in the yearbook room." At this, the goons continued laughing heartily, never losing stride.

"Go fuck yourself in the yearbook room, you dick!" David lunged at Justin, who straightened up and hopped back in shock.

Jess grabbed the back of David's shirt, staring around at the group of nine or ten juniors and seniors who had all along been dying for some dumb freshman to snap and make the first move. "He's sorry!" Jess exclaimed quickly. "He's sick. He didn't mean it." He was struggling to pull David away and continue the other way down the hall.

But Justin was not prepared to let this opportunity escape him. He stepped up and grabbed David's shoulder and forcefully pushed him backward toward the lockers. "What's wrong, buddy?" he asked sardonically, his smile now replaced by an unpleasant sneer that told David his veins were flooding with adrenaline. "We're just trying to help y'all."

"You won't help shit!" David's voice rose frantically, drawing the attention of every student within a twenty-foot radius, who now stood staring at the scene unfolding in the hallway. He was milliseconds away from lunging at Justin again when he heard a teacher from down the hall. "Hey! Stop that!"

Justin's herd had formed a neat semi-circle around the two of them, and crowds were gathering. David wondered how the hyperactive kids who couldn't even walk to lunch in a straight line in first grade held the ability to form perfect circles around the area of a brawl. Justin now lost interest in David and turned toward the teacher with his grinning goons behind him all the while. "Hey, Mr. P.! It's all good over here," his insidious southern drawl assured.

The teacher, whom David had never seen, walked up and motioned for everyone to keep moving. "Let's go! Justin, get to class and quit messing with freshmen."

"You got it, Mr. P." Justin and his goons all walked away and David and Jess turned to go to their lockers.

"Y'all don't even carry books. Stay out of this hall," he told the upperclassmen as they left.

Jess scooted along behind David, who walked mechanically and silently as he stewed in his rage and disappointment, guiding him undisturbed to his locker. "What's going on, David? I've never heard you talk like that before," he said as David broodingly twirled his combination lock.

"Nothing, Jess," David replied through clenched teeth. "I'm just getting sick of all of it, and, unlike you, I'm willing to do something about it."

"Look, if there's something you want to talk about, you know you can tell me, right?"

David slapped his hand on his still unopened locker, creating a slam that attracted the attention of at least fifteen students and the concerned Mr. P., who was still standing some way down the hall with his hands on his hips.

"All right! I'm sorry." Jess turned and walked to his locker, finally leaving David alone. He got his books and hurried away to algebra before Jess could catch up with him.

By the time the bell rang to excuse students for the day, black clouds had formed overhead, and thunder was rumbling in the distance. David looked outside to see autumn leaves whizzing back and forth erratically in the strong wind. When he climbed on the bus, David saw an abrupt flash of lightning and the first drops of rain begin falling from the sky, and he had time to reflect on the aptness of a violent afternoon storm on a day such as this.

David and Jess rode together in complete silence. David sat on the inside staring crossly out the window at the increasingly hard rain and waiting for the next clap of thunder that would break the uncomfortable silence. As the bus rumbled down the long, lonesome road that connected Marlboro Hills with the slightly more urban area of Thriftson County, David struggled to peer into the dense woodlands that surrounded the road on both sides. The afternoon was already nearly as dark as night, rain was coming down in thick sheets that pounded on the glass windows in waves, and each thunderclap was more deafening and abrupt than the last. Frequent flashes of close and violent lightning were all that

allowed David to see into the woods at all; the dreary darkness interrupted by sporadic flashes of thick trees and undergrowth made David
feel more alone than ever. For the first time in a while, he was starting
to feel like his old self again, and he felt embarrassed about how he had
treated Jess and caused such a stupid scene in the hallway.

When the bus turned onto Jess's street and Jess stood up to move
toward the door, David finally glanced over and gave a short, morose
apology: "I'm sorry, Jess. I'll see you tomorrow."

Jess smiled sadly and said, "See ya."

David knew that things would be all right between them by tomorrow. At this point he really would have liked to sit on the curb with Jess
and Megan and see Shaggy again and laugh and mess around like usual,
but when it rained, they didn't bother going outside to meet up. He could
just while away the afternoon reading some of Jess's comics that he hadn't
had much time to look at lately.

He hesitated at the door of the bus for a second, bracing himself
for the torrential wall of rain in front of him, and then made a swift run
toward his front porch, making an effort not to look too desperate and
awkward to the remaining kids on the bus. He leapt up the three steps
and landed on the dry, covered porch by the front door. He was brush-
ing off his hair and shoulders when he heard the crash of his garbage
can being thrown haphazardly back into its usual position at the edge of
his driveway. An ominous voice called out, muffled by the pouring rain.
"You better get outta that house, kid!"

David's heart jumped painfully, his breath halted momentarily,
and his body broke out in chills just from the sheer sound of the voice.
He turned to see a man in a black jumpsuit and an orange vest standing
on the back of a garbage truck that was starting to pull away. He could
clearly hear its loud engine, but he hadn't even noticed it pulling up behind the bus.

"It's bringin' out the worst in ya!" the man called out. David stood
no chance of making out his features at this distance and through all that
liquid interference.

David stood by the door and watched the soaked man standing
weirdly on the back of the truck. As it drove away, the man kept turning toward David, as if to keep his eyes trained on him, until the truck
turned around the corner a block away.

He felt extremely uneasy. Again, he noticed the truck didn't bother stopping at anyone else's house to get their garbage. And what did that guy know about David's house? For the first time, David was genuinely afraid to walk through his front door. It made him a little angry that some sketchy stranger on a garbage truck was the first person to make him seriously consider this situation with his house. David had dismissed Jess and the Stewarts and everyone else who was afraid of this house, but now he was stuck on what some weird garbage man had said? To be fair, the guy did know how to make an impression.

David looked around to see if anyone else was outside, and, seeing no one, went inside and decided that now was a good time to tell his friends everything.

When he walked into the kitchen, he saw two dark silhouettes at the counter, one sitting and the other standing. He reached over and flipped the light switch, but nothing happened; the power was obviously out. Just as his eyes were getting adjusted enough to make out one lumpy silhouette as his father and the other as his mother, lightning lit up the entire house, and then everything was even darker than before. It didn't matter; as soon as he made out his parents sitting there in silence in the still-wrecked kitchen, seemingly waiting for him, everything in his vision went red, as if something in his retinas had burst and filled with blood. The dark shapes in the kitchen were red; what little light came in through the windows was hazed with red. He tried to control himself and stop the overwhelming wave of rage, but he was completely powerless, as though his body were on autopilot while his mind went to the restroom.

"No, thanks. I don't need anything from the store this time. You can put the whole welfare check toward your liquor," David said sardonically.

His father stood up and pushed his mother aside, both somberly silent as though they had been expecting this, waiting for it, waiting for the opportunity to finally put David out of his misery. The worst part was that David didn't care at this point. His mind was blank, gone for the time being; his vision was red, and his body felt like a slingshot drawn back to the max and filled with potential energy.

Pete approached slowly and deliberately while David stood, not moving, and he swung, his fist. David was too quick, though; he bolted aside, grabbed his father's arm, and twisted it around. Pete spun backwards involuntarily, and David punched him directly in the back of the head. Pete fell to the ground and stumbled trying to get back up. David hiked up his leg as high as it would go and then brought it down on his father's back between the shoulders, thrusting his body onto the floor. He grunted as the air whooshed from his fat chest and then screamed so loudly, David actually backed away and winced. Janet came racing forward, shrieking.

"Oh, Petie! You poor thing!" She looked at David with narrowed eyes. "You stay away from him, you shit!" she yelled, obviously afraid of David for once.

David's brain tried to stop him again, but it just seemed to have happened without his say-so. He stormed over toward his mother, and, as she frantically backed away, he jumped into the air. He planted one foot on the edge of the counter to gain more height and power, flew through the air at her, and kicked her in the ribs. She screamed again and fell over on the floor beside David, who landed nimbly on his feet. Pete finally got up and pushed him from behind; David tripped over his fallen mother and landed ungracefully on his stomach, but Pete ignored his squealing wife. He picked David up off the ground by his shirt collar so that his feet were a foot above the floor, reached between his legs, flipped him upside down, and drove his head into the floor like a shovel into frozen earth. David came down so hard on his head that he thought for sure he'd died. The red haze began to fade and gray took over. Before he was completely overcome he staggered dizzily up and kicked his father between the legs, kicked him with all the strength he had left. Pete grabbed at his groin and fell to the floor, nearly puking blood. That was the last that David saw. Faintly, he still heard his mother screaming.

Once again, he came to in his bedroom. Once again, his head hurt quite badly.

14

This was getting out of hand. The sun was shining again, and it looked as though it were about midday. God only knew how many days of school David had missed because of these stupid, reckless brawls. He had to find a way to control his blind hatred toward his parents. He thought about the Stewarts and convinced himself that he had to go see them this weekend. He had to talk to someone about why he was acting like this.

That afternoon David was sitting at his window waiting until he saw the bus drive by so that he could hurry over to Jess's house. Finally, right at four o'clock, the bus drove by, slowed near his driveway, and then carried on down the road. David hurried downstairs and out the door, and rushed over to Jess's house, where he found Jess and Megan sitting together on the porch. Megan looked as though she had been crying, but she stood up hastily and ran to greet him at the sidewalk. This was the first time they had seen each other since their heart-to-heart on the phone, and Megan threw her arms around David, who no longer felt quite frantic enough to resist her touch.

"I've been so worried about you, David," she said after planting a confident and welcome kiss on his cheek, close to his jaw. "We both have."

"I know I've been weird," he said plainly. "I'm so sorry." He wrapped his arms around Megan and squeezed her as tightly as he could without hurting them both, wishing—not for the first time—that they could be together under drastically different circumstances. Maybe one day. She could help him break this curse and they could lead normal lives together until they were old enough to be on their own.

He looked at Jess, who was awkwardly half-sitting, half-standing on his porch steps, and grinned broadly, but Megan was suddenly not grinning at all. "Oh my God! What happened to you?" He hadn't even noticed that the entire left side of his forehead was dark purple with bruises, and he didn't want to know what his head looked like beneath his disheveled hair.

"Look, I need to tell you guys something," David said. They both stared at him, and he took Megan by the hand and led her over toward Jess on the steps. "Ever since I moved into that house, I've been . . . different. And it usually doesn't happen outside the house, just inside, especially when I'm around my parents." They both knew that his parents hated him and were abusive. "When they used to yell and hit me, I just took it, but lately I've been fighting back."

"Well, that's good," said Jess triumphantly.

"No, it isn't good. I mean I haven't just been fighting back. I've been fighting. I actually start fights. Whenever I see them I get really angry, and it's like I see a red haze. I can't stop it. It just overpowers me, and I smart-off to them, and they hit me, and when they hit me, I hit back. It isn't even just hitting anymore, it's crazy." He began speaking quickly and frantically, trying not to let his anxiety overwhelm him and make him cry. "We use objects, like chairs, stools, plates, and sometimes even food. And I even hit my mom." They both got wide-eyed. "I don't mean to, it just happens. The scary part is: I don't even feel sorry for it, but when I leave the house, it's like my anger goes away completely."

"Well, I wouldn't feel sorry for her, either. It's clear she hates you!" Megan said, spreading her arms in David's face as if she was stating what he should already be thinking.

"I know. Maybe it's good. Maybe that's what she gets for making me miserable for all of these years," David said with a small, worried smile spreading across his face. "But, Jess, you saw how I acted yesterday at school. You said yourself that you've never seen me that way before. I don't know what's happening to me, and I'm really worried this house is actually changing me."

Megan held his hand and patted his back until he got himself a little more composed, and then he was able to slow down, start from the beginning, and tell them everything. He told them about Mr. and Mrs. Stewart's visit just after they moved in and about how his sarcastic remarks to his parents had escalated into this monstrous animosity and unease. He told them about the garbage man that yelled at him, and in the end he even told them about his dream from so long ago.

"Well, you can't be sure you even remember all that correctly," Megan said, offering her simple, rational thinking that David had come to respect.

"I know," he said, "But the dream feels right. I had that feeling the first time I saw you. . . and Jess . . . and even Shaggy."

"Well," Megan began again as Jess just sat in an uneasy silence, "I think you're just letting your imagination get carried away. The garbage truck runs here way earlier than four in the afternoon, and that's when you said you saw that garbage man anyway. Are you sure that you aren't just tired? Do you think you've had a concussion or something?"

David felt slightly offended at her suggestions, but he knew that she was probably right. He was likely to have suffered ample brain injuries lately to make him feel this paranoid, but Jess finally chimed in before he could respond.

"I think you have to get out of that house," he said. "I don't know how, but you don't need to be staying there. It's cursed."

"Come on, Jess," Megan said, rushing to get him to stop talking before David could get upset again.

"I'm sorry! I don't like it any more than you do, but something is off about it. You know the legends as well as I do. It's evil."

"That's just a story, Jess. A house can't be evil."

"But everyone who's ever lived there has either died or gone insane. That house is evil," Jess maintained.

"Look at David's parents!" Megan said. "They aren't breaking down. It's just David, because stuff like this is stressing him out so much!"

"I'm still here," David reminded them, feeling oddly singled-out.

"Yeah, but . . . " Jess paused, "I guess it works differently on different people. I guess some people gradually go insane, but not all the family members. I don't know why, but it just always turns out that way, and eventually all of them suffer."

"Suffer?" David asked.

"Well, look at you. Everyone in that house is obviously more miserable than they were before. I'm telling you, you need to get out."

Megan started to argue with Jess further, but David interrupted. "Look, I've decided that I'm going to go see the Stewarts tomorrow afternoon. They are obviously not crazy—or at least not any crazier than anyone else who believes this crap—and they have probably lived here a while. I'm sure they can help me figure something out." This seemed to satisfy both Megan and Jess, because Megan relaxed her hand on David's, and Jess didn't say anything else until he stood up and opened his front door.

"Oh," he said as Shaggy ran out. "I totally forgot about you, boy."

Shaggy ran and jumped immediately in David's lap, and his comforting wet nose and tongue almost set his mind at ease as much as Megan's warm hand in his own. The four of them sat around for another hour or so just shooting the breeze before Jess announced that he needed to go in for dinner soon. He patted David's back, wished him luck, and turned to go inside. "I'll see you tomorrow."

"Okay. Bye," David replied, smiling.

David and Megan sat on the porch in an awkward silence for a few moments after Jess closed the door, Megan looking at the street and David petting Shaggy, who was lying between his legs. People say that at that age, one can't understand what love is, but David was pretty sure he understood. He understood just fine. Some believe that one must feel heartbreak to understand and appreciate love, but David had never felt love toward anyone else in his life, and he was sure that he loved Megan and Jess. He desperately wanted to remind her how grateful he was to have her in his life, but what he really wanted to say was that he loved her. He, in his naiveté, felt pretty sure that she loved him back, but he was too afraid of being shunned nonetheless. He wanted her to know that she made all the difference between the crap excuse for living that he had previously known and his wonderful new ideas of the present. When he finally looked up, he saw a mixture of sadness and longing in Megan's eyes that made him love her even more. His stomach tightened with excitement and emotion, and, without thinking, he leaned toward her and quickly kissed her on the lips. He saw her mouth quiver when he pulled away, and then her eyes narrowed in a sad look of confusion.

"What was that for?" she asked, and David could only shrug in embarrassment. "Well, why did you do it?" she asked again, not unkindly.

"I just . . . it just happened," David stammered.

"It just seemed weird." She sat contemplating for a second. "No, I didn't mean that. It's just that it was—"

"I know. I'm sorry."

"I didn't mean it like that, David," she insisted, but he wasn't ready to give her a chance to explain. This was his greatest fear, and his euphoria came crashing down around him. He stood up and began walking with Shaggy back toward his house muttering piteous farewells.

"David! I was trying to say that it was too short!" she called, "I didn't understand why you did it and then immediately pulled away." He turned back to face her, savoring the feeling of relief that made his shaky knees once again stable, and smiled slowly. Megan smiled too, her bright eyes shining in the dim light, and waved a hand to him. "Goodnight, David," she said coyly. He walked slowly and wordlessly away, feeling slightly confused, yet excited.

15

Friday after school, Jess asked David if he was going to ask Megan to come to their school's Halloween dance; she went to a private school, but she would be allowed to come as long as she had an invitation.

"Ha! Yeah, right. That's how we want to spend Halloween—at some stupid dance with everyone from school."

Jess looked momentarily crestfallen. "Oh, yeah. I was just curious. I probably won't go, either."

David glanced over at Jess, read the disappointment in his eyes, and was suddenly sorry that he had been so quick to scoff at the suggestion. In actuality, David had always loved going to his old middle school's dances, even when he had no one to hang out with and no date. Now that he had both, he was becoming cold and cynical; he could tell that he had hurt Jess's feelings, but the thought of going to that stupid dance made him feel sick to his stomach. When he looked up and saw Megan coming around the corner and Shaggy speeding frantically down the sidewalk to greet her, he secretly hoped that Jess never mentioned the dance again, especially in front of her. If she actually wanted to go, he didn't know what he would do.

The three of them spent the afternoon talking and laughing like usual, and no one even mentioned David's recent darker days or his plan to visit the Stewarts later that evening. Before he stood up to leave, though, he let both of them know that he would talk to them on Saturday and let them know what Mr. and Mrs. Stewart had said. He beckoned a panting Shaggy to follow him home and bid his two friends good-evening, not quite feeling confident enough to steal a kiss from Megan with Jess still present.

David reached his house a few moments later, snuck Shaggy upstairs to lock him in his room, grabbed his coat, and set off again out the door. Night was falling, and, being the middle of October, it was getting cool out.

He walked across the street and neared the Stewarts' front porch. Their house looked to David just like all the other houses in the neighborhood. He turned back momentarily and studied his house from afar. It looked the same as ever before. Aside from a few minute defining features like those that any house in a suburban neighborhood possessed (the foggy scar on the top left corner of the tiny attic window, the out-of-place fresh layer of paint over just the railing of the small front porch, the round stained-glass window above the garage door, the birdlike shapes carved at the top of the posts holding the awning over the porch), David's house did not seem significant or out of place at all, and it definitely didn't seem evil. As David started to turn back toward the Stewarts' house, however, he noticed the two upstairs windows giving off an odd, dim, red glow like the foreboding eyes of a demonic caricature, but when he quickly snapped his head back around to look again, the windows were as they always had been. Dim yellow lamplight shined out of David's upstairs bedroom window while the adjacent bathroom window was dark. When he turned back around again and saw the red gleam of the setting sun on the horizon, he felt pretty confident that he had pinpointed the source of the windows' red glow.

He sighed and continued up the walkway and onto the Stewarts' porch. A light was on inside, but the curtains were drawn. David could hear the television playing in the living room, and he imagined the kindly couple sitting at the dining room table, eating and watching television, both happy. Happy until he knocked on the door, that is.

David stood on the porch for a long while, contemplating just turning back and going home. He wasn't sure if he should be here bothering them, and he had no idea what he intended to tell them or ask of them. Then he remembered Mr. Stewart's telling him to come over as soon as possible if he ever needed help. He remembered the scared look in his eyes and the way he seemed to know something that he did not tell, almost as if he expected David to come by soon anyway, as if he were already waiting for David.

When he finally knocked, a streetlight came on behind him and the door opened. Mrs. Stewart stood in the doorway, looking positively content, but when she saw who it was, the pleased look on her face turned to concern.

"Oh, come in, please," she said abruptly.

"Oh, thank you," David replied, stepping inside and feeling very rushed and intrusive. "I just wanted to talk to you and your husband for a bit and maybe get your opinions about some things."

The fear and concern in her eyes swiftly turned to despair, and she tilted her head contemplatively to one side and broke her eye contact. David stepped inside, and she closed the door behind him.

"Who's there, hon?" called a deeper voice from the kitchen—Mr. Stewart's voice. They went into the dining room and Mrs. Stewart pulled a chair out from under the table for David.

"It's David," she said urgently.

Like a flash, Mr. Stewart was coming around the corner and approaching the table where David had sat. "What's wrong? What is it?" he cried.

David was trying to remain calm, but their behavior was unnerving. "What makes you think something is wrong?"

"Oh, I'm sure of it. Halloween is approaching, and now you're coming to ask our help. We've been here long enough to know that isn't a coincidence."

David, who was quickly abandoning what little agenda he had devised while standing on their front porch, could not help but pursue such an unsettling statement. "What's going to happen on Halloween?" he asked, not even fully understanding the question.

"There's no telling!" Mr. Stewart replied exasperatedly. "I thought that's what you've come to let us know!"

David was thoroughly at a loss for words. He opened his mouth to inquire further, but he had no idea what to ask. He glanced over at Mrs. Stewart, who was standing at the other end of the table and staring at him as though he had some grotesque and fatal disfigurement. She could obviously detect David's unease. "Oh, Walt, don't scare the boy, now. Let's just hear what he came to tell us before we start making assumptions. We don't know that there's necessarily anything wrong."

"I'm telling you, this isn't right," Mr. Stewart countered, giving David no chance to interject, "But fine, let's just hear what he came to say." They both looked severely at David and waited for him to gather his words.

The image of this neighborly couple bickering like old birds made David feel even worse than their frantic demeanor did. He looked back and forth at both of them and decided that he would submit. "Well, actually, yes, there is something I was wondering. You seemed to know more than you told me that first night I met you, in August. When I go into that house now, I feel . . . different, and when I see my parents, I get angry. I see a red haze, and I just go crazy. I start hitting them and yelling just like they've always done to me." He assumed that they had already guessed that bit of trivia about his parents, and he was picking up steam now, slipping into the spreading hysteria. "I've gotten stronger too. I can almost beat up my dad. I'm doing things that I've never even seen before, fighting like a trained professional! I'll just wake up and go downstairs, and when I see my parents, we fight, and it's like I have some new technique every time."

As David spoke faster and faster, Mr. and Mrs. Stewart never looked away from his face. They both looked extremely scared, absolutely terrified and revolted by what he was telling them, and yet they both seemed to be utterly captivated by his outlandish recounting.

"Oh, dear," Mrs. Stewart said at last. "It's happened again."

16

"What?" David asked. "What's happened?"

"Well," Mr. Stewart began in his slow, southern drawl, "I guess I'll have to start from the beginning." He paused and sat contemplatively for a moment before moving on. "About thirty years ago, when my wife and I were just married and settling in here, a man named Frank Batterman came to town and decided to clear off a bunch of land and build a house. This here was the only house in the area then. We bought it, and it was surrounded by woods. Well, Mr. Batterman bought up a bunch of that land from us with a price that we newlyweds just could not refuse, and he cleared out those woods just to build his one house a few feet away over there. He was crazy, determined, and zealous. I don't know how he ever came about to be such a successful businessman, but, anyway, he planted grass all over where he cleared the land and built that house right across the street, which used to be a little dirt road. He lived in it for a few years and hardly ever came out.

"After that, most of this neighborhood was being built outward from our two houses, and people started moving in. The roads were being paved, and houses were being constructed day in and day out. Once the whole neighborhood was built, things were quiet for a while. But then some of the new residents started disappearing. There were search parties, but no one was ever found. After a while, the police just gave up. Stuff like that just kind of dies down when it isn't solved, you know? But still it kept happening. People kept turning up missing. No one suspected Frank—but then again, no one really ever suspected anyone," he paused, recollecting his thoughts. "Or perhaps everyone suspected everyone. Who knows? Either way, no one ever saw Frank out of his house. After something like thirty people disappeared in five months, the police began to become irritated, if you can imagine. They started questioning everyone everywhere, eventually going around door-to-door asking questions. They didn't find any answers, though. No one knew what was going on. They had squad cars circling the neighborhood all day and night. All night they'd go around with their spotlights shining in windows and between houses. They searched the woods, the rivers, the lakes. Everywhere! It got so out-of-hand that cops started standing post at nearly every corner; at the end of one's field of vision stood another, then another, then another. Seemed like every officer on duty was in this very neighborhood. There was no way they could miss anything. But people continued to disappear, and the police continued to find out nothing.

"Now, every serial killer has his flaw, and Batterman's was that he continued to kill even when it was almost impossible not to get caught. Yes, he kept on killing, and eventually, the police saw him out one night. He was on the very edge of the neighborhood, coming out of the woods that still surround the place. They go on for many, many miles. The exact number is unknown to me. I'm not even sure what's at the other end. Anyway, Frank was coming out of those woods, on the side farthest from town, when someone saw him. He was covered in dirt and blood. A few cops approached him, and he was smiling—laughing! He didn't say anything, but he reached behind his back and pulled out a grotesque-looking double-sided axe. Mr. Batterman began swinging that axe and doing a whole bunch of crazy stuff, yelling and cussing at the top of his lungs. He managed to kill probably ten or fifteen cops one at a time just by running down the streets taking one out before he could warn the others that something was going on. Apparently the first guy who saw him radioed the others about someone suspicious coming out of the woods, but Batterman took out half of the friggin' neighborhood before anyone realized what was happening. Finally someone shot him in the legs and brought him down.

"There was a hell of a cleanup after that. They took him in for interrogation, and he just kept muttering something about the ground by the bare side of a pine tree. Everybody knows that those woods are filled with oak trees and oak trees only. Right after he mentioned this, he entered a severe catatonic state and never said anything else for the rest of his life. They took him down to the mental institution where he was fed from tubes until he died of old age, just a few years ago.

"Well, ever since that horrific night, every time someone new moves into that Batterman house, something bad happens. No one knows exactly what happens or how it happens, but it sure enough does, and before it's all over with, all the family members are dead and gone too. The same two things never happen twice, though, 'cause people should catch on and put a stop to it, but people always disappear, and everyone knows they're dead, and just before the psycho victim enters that catatonic stage for eternity, he mentions something about that same damn pine tree."

David was completely astonished. Astonished wouldn't even begin to describe how he felt. He was absolutely flabbergasted. He looked at Mrs. Stewart and she just nodded.

"Why don't they just tear down the house?" he asked.

"Why would someone destroy a house in the middle of a quiet neighborhood?"

"Well, if it's cursed . . ."

"And who is going to be bold enough to say that a house is cursed?" asked Mr. Stewart matter-of-factly.

"But . . ." David was at a loss for words. "Everyone here says it's cursed! Why would anyone buy it?"

"Why wouldn't they? It's just a house. Just a local legend." David was starting to feel like Mr. Stewart was playing a game. "Look, I'm the only one who takes the time to put the pieces together. I've been here from the beginning, and no one else sees any connection. All they see is families coming and going. It looks completely normal."

"Disappearances and brutal murders look normal?" David asked incredulously.

"No one sees that. After Batterman thirty years ago, there were no deaths or showdowns for the public to witness, and not one of the thirty or so victims has ever been found."

He thought hard, and couldn't understand how something like this could be real, how any one person could believe it was real, but he also thought of how the curse had crossed his mind several times over the past few months. David wanted to run. He wanted to get away from this place as fast as possible, but he knew he couldn't. Where would he go? What would he do? If this was true, he would find a way to beat this thing. He was determined to stop these feelings he'd been having.

"What should I do?" he asked finally. "What should I do to stop this?"

"We don't have any idea," Mrs. Stewart said somberly. "We may never understand what exactly is going on in that house."

David felt suddenly helpless. He had thought this wise old couple would have been able to help him stop whatever was going on. "But you said I could come to you if I needed anything," he pleaded.

Mr. and Mrs. Stewart sat somberly for a moment and seemed to be thinking what to say.

"I'd say just stay out of that house and away from your parents as much as possible," Mr. Stewart finally concluded. "Although we've never been able to help anyone else that's lived there, you came to us, and I have faith that you will be able to put an end to this dreadful curse."

17

As David walked back home and began getting ready for bed, he took pause once more to examine the façade of his legendary house. Even knowing what he did now, nothing stood out to him. No solution seemed within grasp. He felt mentally numb after talking with Mr. and Mrs. Stewart, and the sight of his house still frightened him much less than it probably should.

Though he was relieved to know the whole backstory to the legend of his house, he couldn't bring himself to shrug it off any longer. He knew that he didn't possess the characteristics to be a psycho serial killer like Mr. Batterman, but he also knew that he had been acting out of character and out of control a lot lately, and as hard as it might be to believe, he had to accept that this house must be having some effect on his mind. He decided that he was going to do what Mr. Stewart had suggested, and that he was going to tell his friends about their discussion as soon as possible.

The next day he told Jess and Megan everything that Mr. Steward said, and, to his surprise, they seemed almost amused. "Why do you look so content?" he asked when he finished.

"Come on," Megan said. "It's just some story."

"If it's just some story, why don't you two ever come into my house?" David asked.

"Because it would just be awkward. I wouldn't want to be around your parents." Megan must have known this wouldn't hurt David's feelings. Despite the fact that she was trying to set him at ease, David was getting a little irritated.

"And what about you, Jess? You said that first day that the house made you feel different."

Jess seemed to be in agreement, but torn between what things to say.

"Oh, come on, that's just make-believe," Megan snapped at their childishness.

"But I've started fighting back. I've started standing up to my parents." Now David almost wanted to believe that the curse was real and that he could overcome it. "What if that house is making me lose my mind?"

"Yes, and you've started having friends. You've started growing up. It's not that abnormal. You've just grown sick of the things they do. Look on the bright side. They've managed to keep you alive, and they've managed to keep you healthy. In just a few years, you can leave them for good. You're only fighting now because you believe that you can." David loved her more and more with every word that she spoke. She could flawlessly uncover every discrepancy in Mr. Stewart's story and every concern that had arisen in David's mind, simply using logic.

He smiled at her. "I guess you're right, but it's probably still a good idea for me to try and do something about it, don't you think?"

"It can't hurt," Megan conceded. "Every second away from your parents would do you some good."

"I know it sounds silly," David admitted, "But I don't want to go crazy. I would rather just stay away from the house."

When everyone was in agreement, they decided that he was going to start sleeping out of the house.

Megan and Jess waited on the curb while David walked over to convey their plans to the Stewarts. They had told him before he left the previous night that he should feel free to drop by if he needed anything else, or even if he just wanted something to do. They had plenty of free time and plenty of handy stuff.

Mr. Stewart was ecstatic about the idea of moving out of the house without actually moving out, and David was too kind to admit that he was now beginning to think that the poor man and his wife were suffering from strange delusions. Mr. Stewart was more than happy to lend David an old tent. It was the most bizarre thing that David could have ever imagined, almost like a circus tent. It was a massive, jungle-green canvas that looked like something from the army.

David took the tent back to his house, and Megan and Jess came over to help. They wouldn't go inside the house; they just helped him set up the canvas in his front yard and arrange everything inside. They moved David's clothes and Shaggy's bed and toys into it. David was surprised to find he could actually stand upright in the grotesquely oversized abode. It was large enough to move David's twin-size bed into. David struggled on his own to tilt the heavy mattress and box spring onto their sides and slide them down the stairs and maneuver them around the corners one at a time, but they stacked quite neatly on one side of the tent. All of his major belongings that they could possibly fit, they did. The only reason David would need to go inside would be to eat, shower, and groom; he felt a strong sensation of triumph very unlike his most recent victorious feelings after delivering blows and insults to his parents.

He felt confident that his parents wouldn't say a word about his sleeping in the yard. They hardly ever talked to him at all anymore; he thought that they were actually afraid of him now.

When they'd finished with the tent, they went back to the curb and sat down in their usual spot.

"We really need to find a way to keep all of my stuff safe," David said.

"Yeah, but this is a pretty friendly neighborhood. I think we're about the only kids here. Other than the little kids all over the place, of course, but they won't bother anything," Megan said.

"That's true," David agreed. "Plus, I really only have books and blankets in there." There was a momentary contemplative silence, then David said, "So I don't really need anything electrical, but how will I keep warm?" Winter was just around the corner, and while Alabama stayed suffocatingly hot during the summer and fall, winter nights and mornings could be uncomfortably cool.

"Well, you have two big blankets right now. That will keep you warm until you can talk to Mr. Stewart and maybe buy some sort of heater that you can use out there before it gets too cold," Megan assured him.

"Right." David thought they had pretty much covered everything. He didn't indulge in frivolities such as television or computers, so he had no need for electricity, and a simple battery-powered book light would keep him content and entertained after dark.

"Tomorrow we have to go back to school," Jess said, abruptly ending the silence. "That stinks."

"Yep," David agreed. He knew they were both dreading Justin's gang of bullies, who were undoubtedly still steaming from their last interrupted engagement.

"I know this is all really hard on you," Jess began, just as abruptly. He paused, looking a little uncomfortable about carrying on. "But do you ever think about, like . . . uncovering the mystery behind the house?"

"I don't know," David replied plainly and honestly.

Jess continued. "Maybe one day we'll discover the secrets about Mr. Batterman and that curse."

"Maybe," David said noncommittally. He smiled weakly as he considered the profound sense of wonder and adventure that such a squirrelly kid as Jess could possess.

As night began to fall, they went their separate ways, Jess and Megan to their homes and David to his new home, but only after obtaining a thick army sleeping bag and an old, expensive-looking fuel- and battery-powered space heater from an excessively eager Mr. Stewart.

18

Staying in the tent was most definitely the best idea that David had ever had. Over the next few days he and his father tussled once or twice; David would shoot some sarcastic remark at an unsuspecting Pete, who would react by looking incredulous as ever, and the two would engage in a verbal standoff resulting in each party leaving in opposite directions mumbling hatefully to himself. Few punches were thrown, and after a few days, David no longer felt the urge to antagonize his parents. Even when he was in the house with them, those feelings had begun to die down a little. Perhaps spending time away from them really had made them seem less threatening. David thought that he was going to be able to beat Mr. Stewart's curse of the Batterman house and his own curse of the Slate house after all.

He never asked Megan to the Halloween dance at his school. They just sat out in his tent and talked on Halloween night. Jess had to sit at home with his parents, who apparently felt that he was too old to go trick-or-treating yet too immature to refrain from being mischievous; being out and wandering around on Halloween night could be dangerous to him as well as to others. They had no clue who their son really was, but what parents do? David, however, didn't give Jess too much grief about this, as he knew it would buy him some time alone with Megan.

Megan was sitting on David's mattress in the tent, drumming her fingers anxiously on her legs while David dragged Shaggy around in circles as he clung to a stuffed cat. "It's weird not having Jess around," she said finally.

David's flesh suddenly got very hot, as he knew that she was beating around some bush, and that was very unlike her. "Yeah," he agreed absentmindedly, willing her to drop another hint.

"When was the last time it was just me and you?" she asked rhetorically. "I guess we haven't really been alone that often." Then she paused dramatically. "It's nice."

"Yeah," David agreed again, feeling awkward and ineloquent. Megan sighed at his response, and he hoped that she knew he was following her. He wished that he could just tell her that he knew where she was going but that the thought of kissing her again was sending him into a mental and verbal coma.

"So what do you want to do?" she asked finally, showing her first signs of impatience.

Kiss you, David thought, imagining himself pushing her backwards on the bed and crawling on top of her with his lips against hers.

"I don't know," he said lamely. "What do we usually do?"

Megan shrugged and rolled her eyes.

"Erm," David tried to begin, but he could think of nothing to say. Was Jess really this vital to his relationship with Megan?

As if she were reading his mind, Megan asked, "Why is this so awkward without Jess?"

"I don't know," David lamely admitted.

Realizing that talking wasn't going to get her anywhere with David this evening, Megan leaned in and pressed her lips to the corner of his mouth, but instead of instantly pulling away as he had done, she kept her face next to his, and she even grabbed his cheek and pulled his head closer to hers so that their lips were stuck together like two symmetrical magnets. Bursts of light and sound were going off in David's head like fireworks. He almost couldn't even enjoy the kiss through all the distractions in his head, but after a few seconds Megan finally pulled away. David took two deep breaths, got his heart rate under control, and snaked his arm underneath hers so that he could wrap it around her back and pull her in again.

This time he opened his mouth a little and allowed his lips to investigate hers. This kiss he fully relished and absorbed, thinking of nothing but how wonderful her face felt next to his. Thank God for dominant women like Megan, or guys like David would have died out millennia ago.

19

The beginning of November went about the same as the end of October. David stayed in the tent except when he needed to take a shower or eat. He eventually started eating inside rather than taking the food out to his tent. When Janet or Pete walked through the kitchen, they merely glanced at David, who would just continue eating; none of the three seemed to care at all about the others' existence any longer. He didn't get feelings of rage or angst at all any more, and he was never engulfed in that red haze of hatred. In fact, he thought he was completely back to his normal self now.

Late one afternoon at the very beginning of the Thanksgiving holiday, David was sitting on the curb outside his tent with Shaggy at his side when he heard the increasing pitch of an approaching truck. The afternoon sun was setting in the west, and Megan and Jess had recently left his company for the evening, leaving him to sit alone, tossing a stick for Shaggy to fetch and return to him and reflecting on the newfound comfort and happiness that he had finally managed to find in his life.

David looked up as the rumble of the truck's engine got louder and nearer. It sounded like a very large truck that was approaching with dangerous speed. When the dark blue truck finally turned the corner onto Jade Street about three blocks away from David's house, he saw that it wasn't a huge truck at all; only its tires were disproportionately large, and it was just the exhaust pipes that were big and loud. The truck sped along the street toward David, completely ignoring two stop signs and growing deafeningly loud as the engine sputtered and roared, ever nearer. David squeezed Shaggy's collar to ensure that he didn't run into the street and get crushed under the truck's oversized tires, but Shaggy only stared uncomfortably at the source of the noise. David stared, too, as it roared past him, but the windows were all nearly completely blacked out, and he could see no one inside.

When it passed, he stood up and walked with Shaggy back toward the tent, but the driver of the truck had slammed on the brakes and stopped in the middle of the street. David froze and looked uneasy as the passenger window rolled down and a familiar sneering, unfriendly face peered back at him. The reverse lights came on at the back of the truck, and David quickly kept walking to his tent. He scooped Shaggy inside and stood up straight to look as one of Justin Guy's usual goons said, "Hey, ol' buddy! Where you hurrying off to?"

David's heart started beating much too fast as the truck stopped rolling backwards at the edge of his driveway and he saw Justin Guy himself at the wheel. He zipped the door of the tent closed so that Shaggy couldn't get out and managed to stutter weakly, "Uh, n-nowhere." A tight knot had coiled in his stomach and seemed to be snaking its way up his throat; he could feel the thick lump back there, causing his breathing to become uneven and his speech forced.

Both doors of the truck opened as Justin and Robbie Traywick, a sweaty senior with far too much facial hair, stepped out and started walking unceremoniously toward David in his own front yard. "What's this?" Justin chimed in his brash Southern tongue. "You campin' out with Benji?"

David stepped backwards warily, almost wishing that he wasn't so much back to his usual timid self at this particular moment. "Yeah," he tried to smile and laugh in a friendly way. "I guess you could say that."

"Aw, man, ain't that just too cute? Why weren't we invited?" They kept walking closer to him, both smiling balefully.

David didn't know what to say. He took one last small step back and stopped when his heel touched the bottom of the tent.

"Where's mommy and daddy?" Justin continued, as if David had responded as amicably as ever.

"Um . . . " David's nerves were shot, and his body was limp and useless, but his intellect started to kick in again, at least a little, "They're just inside. Probably washing dishes or something."

"Yeah, right," Justin said, reaching out and grabbing David's shirt collar. "They'd prob'ly do this to you too, you greasy faggot."

Before he was slung helplessly to the ground like a rag-doll, David had a flashing, wild image of himself making a mad dash for his front door, stepping in, and leaping back outside filled with energy, rage, and power. This fleeting notion vanished well before his head hit the ground mere inches away from his concrete driveway. Afterwards, David didn't say or think much of anything at all. He winced and groaned when Robbie's steel-toed work boots slammed into his ribs and stomach, and he cried out when Justin lifted him back off the ground to get a few facial shots in. Yes, he was pretty well back to his old self, after all.

"Come on, pussy! You ain't so tough now without teachers around to protect you, are ya?"

WHAM! Justin's curled fist smacked David high on the cheekbone, whipping his head to one side and causing blood to trickle from his left nostril.

"Nothing good to say now?" David obviously made an exquisite punching bag for Justin; he was not trying to fight back or even to defend himself. His arms hung limply at his side, though his mind, unfortunately, was still conscious. Justin held David upright and allowed himself one more solid jab, straight to the side of the nose, simultaneously letting go of David's shirt and allowing the blow to send him forcefully back to the grass. "Well, I think you've fuckin' said enough anyway, bitch!" Justin's accent made "think" sound like "thank," and David's frazzled brain was momentarily confused as to why he was being thanked at a time like this. His limp body hit the ground one last time and bounced. He lay motionless, staring at the close-up blades of grass and barely holding on to consciousness as Justin and Robbie continued to heckle him while looking around suspiciously to be sure that no one had witnessed their assault.

"We'll see who's fuckin' themself in the yearbook room."

"He'll cradle his boyfriend's balls in the yearbook room."

When they finally got back into Justin's truck, which was left running the whole time, and drove away, David allowed his eyes to close and his familiar tears of self-pity to come. Lying beaten in the middle of his yard in a sizable neighborhood before dark, he wondered how many of his neighbors had been walking to their mailboxes or peering out their windows or front doors as Justin and Robbie bruised his ribs and back again and again with their steel-toed boots. He wondered angrily how many Neutrals had stood by and done nothing while he got clobbered in plain sight in an unfair fight that he had never even wanted in the first place. Finally, he wondered if his own parents had happened to look out the window and had maybe stopped to watch the show as their own son was beaten to a pulp in their front yard.

After several minutes he found the strength to drag his aching body to the tent, unzip the door, and curl up on his mattress to cry himself to sleep with a concerned-looking Shaggy at his side.

20

The next afternoon, Megan and Jess were far from pleased to hear David's humiliating account of the previous evening's events. Megan had been spared many of the details, and David refrained from lifting his shirt to reveal the countless bruises while she was around, but Jess was brooding darkly over Justin's ballsy public attack.

"I can't believe he would just come into your yard and hit you like that, and in broad daylight!" he exclaimed.

"Yeah, David. You should call the police or something. That's just crazy," Megan added.

"What would calling the police accomplish?" David asked darkly. "They would do virtually nothing aside from making him even angrier at me . . . and now he knows where I live."

They sat for a few more minutes in silence, no one quite daring to suggest that it might be safer for David to move back into his house after this regrettable occurrence, until Jess glumly announced that he should be getting home. After this Megan left too, her mood also a bit dour.

Justin's interference made David's entire situation decisively more complicated. Staying outside for these few short weeks had helped tremendously with his family problems, and it obviously was helping with his mental state outside of home, but living on his lawn in a tent now seemed more dangerous than ever. He thought that Jess and Megan were, on some level, accepting defeat after they had gotten such high hopes of David's ending the curse, and he too was feeling a bit helpless.

The next evening David and Megan managed to find a bit of time together without Jess tagging along, and they sat on the curb talking, as usual.

"So you and your parents don't fight any more, right?"

"Nope, we've hardly said one word to each other since I put the tent up."

"That's great," she said, trying to sound genuine. "I can't believe you may have figured out a way to get rid of that stinking curse." She smiled at her own raillery.

"Yeah, well," David didn't want to jinx his late success, "I don't think I'm getting rid of the curse. I think I'm just . . . postponing it or something." He got chills at the thought.

"Good grief. I wasn't being serious." She raised her voice, "There is no curse!" Then she seemed to second-guess her method, judging by the look of the uncertainty on David's face. "Well, whatever you're doing, keep it up. It seems to be working out pretty well."

"Yeah, but I was thinking—just for experimental purposes—that I should move back into the house." David put a hand on her shoulder as Megan's eyes widened, but he noticed that she didn't look altogether surprised. "Calm down. I just want to see if the urges start to come back. If they do, then I'll go right back to the tent. I just hate it out here. I can't eat or shower or get ready for school or anything any more. Plus, sleeping on the floor gets kind of old after a month, and now I have to worry about being ambushed when I'm least expecting it. I can't live like that." He frowned. "If you really think there's no curse, we should have nothing to worry about, right?"

"David," she seemed hurt, "It's not really that I don't think it exists at this point. It's just that I don't want to believe in it." He began to feel ill. It hurt more than he would have predicted for her to stop maintaining the truth of what she had been saying all along. Although he still imagined the curse as a physical being, he, too, wanted to believe in Megan's logic. If she couldn't even truly believe it, how could he? Where would he be now without Megan's stern insistence that he had nothing to worry about? "I think you'd better ask Mr. and Mrs. Stewart first."

David thought for a minute, trying not to become openly upset. "All right, I'll ask them, but I don't think that they're going to like it very much. I'll sleep in the tent tonight, and tomorrow I'll go over and talk to them."

They kissed, as they often did now when Jess wasn't around, and Megan got up to leave.

"Wait," David started.

Megan turned around. "What is it?"

"Well, I just wanted to tell you . . ." He paused for too long.

"Tell me what?"

"Um . . . n—never mind."

"No, tell me." She looked worried.

"Well," David looked up from the floor, "I . . . love you." His heart leapt wildly as the weight of those words flew from his heart to hers.

Megan smiled, and he saw that her worry had vanished completely. It was the smile she had the first day they met. He loved that smile, and he thought that its timely revisit could mean that perhaps she had loved him on that first day too. He thought he saw her eyes begin to water.

"I . . . er . . . you really mean a lot to me. I don't know what I would do without you or Jess."

"I love you too, David," she paused. "I'd better get home now." She leaned in one last time and kissed him on the corner of the mouth, very affectionately.

"Okay. Bye," he said, smiling like a goon. All things considered, he felt pretty good after their discussion, and knowing that he now had a goal seemed to help a bit, as well.

After Megan left, he got up and walked out of the tent. He felt sad that she left so abruptly after his confession, but it made the moment more awkward. More special. More memorable.

It had just gotten dark, and a streetlight popped on. He saw Megan walking home in its light. Watching her leave, he could have done a dance right there in the yard, but he restrained himself.

He walked into the house to brush his teeth, and his mother was in the kitchen. She looked at him, for the first time since their first night there, the way she had always looked at him since the day he was born. At first David felt scared and sad like he always used to feel when receiving that look, but then he felt a little relieved. His parents must have realized that he was back to normal again, because his mother actually spoke to him. She spoke to him like any other time.

"Tomorrow is Wednesday. You need to take the garbage out in the morning."

He was absolutely astounded, but he managed to reply, "Okay."

He walked upstairs, half happy and relieved, half worried and confused, and brushed his teeth. Since he'd promised Megan that he would stay in the tent again tonight, he went back outside and lay down. He clicked the bright little book light closed and leaned back in his sleeping bag on top of his mattress, thinking of what he would do and what may happen when he did it. He wasn't sure if he liked staying in the tent and being tormented by his parents all over again more than staying in the house and beating them to a pulp every time their eyes met. He considered the latter more appealing, but he shuddered at the thought of what may happen if he kept it that way for long enough.

21

David awoke late Wednesday just after noon feeling a bit nervous about what he was planning to do. He went inside, took a shower and got dressed, then went downstairs and got a bowl out of the cabinet to pour cereal. He glanced at the clock on the wall, which read twenty-four past one, and wondered why he had slept so late. He guessed it was because he was up late with Megan the night before.

Yeah, that's it. I was up later than usual last night, and I slept later than usual this morning . . . nothing weird about that.

When David finished his cereal and put the bowl in the sink, he grabbed his shoes and walked outside. He sat down on the front steps and put them on, then walked across the street to the Stewarts' house and knocked on the door. Mr. Stewart answered and gestured David inside.

"Come in and have some tea," he said.

"Oh, thanks."

Since their discussion about Frank Batterman, David had visited Mr. and Mrs. Stewart numerous times. If Megan or Jess weren't around and he got bored, he and Shaggy would walk across the street to talk with one or both of their friendly neighbors. Mr. Stewart was always welcoming, and he always bade David to return. They usually sat in the kitchen or living room and drank tea or ate various snacks. The Stewarts had better junk food than David had ever imagined existed, and he liked being able to eat snacks and feel like a normal kid. Since he had none at home, he had started to view Mr. and Mrs. Stewart as parent figures, as mentors. They always asked David questions about himself, a topic about which his parents never seemed to care, and David asked them questions in return: questions about their past, about their friends, about their family, about their plans. On one occasion when Mrs. Stewart was away shopping, David asked Mr. Stewart if they had any children nearby. Immediately grateful that he just happened to ask when Mrs. Stewart was away,

David found out that they had lost three children before deciding to give up completely. They were all named James, after Mr. Stewart's father. The topic obviously upset Mrs. Stewart greatly.

"Please don't mention it in front of Jean. She's suffered quite a lot over the years because of it."

"Oh, of course," David had assured him. He had also learned their first names, Jean and Walter, but he never called them that.

They walked inside, and David sat down at the dining room table. Mr. Stewart called for his wife and then joined David with glasses of sweet tea for both of them. At first, David had found their sense of urgency and inseparability amusing, but it eventually became a little annoying having them both get so serious and concerned every time he visited. He realized that he just had to accept some of the strange quirks of the elderly.

"I'm coming!" Mrs. Stewart yelled back through the hallway, and soon she joined them in the dining room with a glass of tea for herself.

"Well, I see that the tent is still in your yard." They both seemed much calmer this time than they tended to be. They already seemed to know that things had gotten better. "Is everything still working out?"

"It's going great," David said genuinely. "I've lost all urges to start anything with my parents. There've been no more fights, and I'm even starting to feel normal when I'm inside the house with them. My mom even talked to me last night the way she used to."

Oh, Christ—the trash. Maybe I can get it tonight.

"In fact, things are going so well, that I was wondering if you thought it would be a good idea if I moved back into the house." He hastily added, "If I got any of those feelings again, I would come right back out and try something else, but sleeping on the ground for a month isn't that much fun. It starts to get to you after a few weeks." His rationalizations seemed transparent as he recited them to Mr. and Mrs. Stewart, but he was determined not to upset them or the infirm balance of his universe by mentioning what had recently happened with Justin and Robbie.

The Stewarts pondered this suggestion for a few moments in silence, then Mrs. Stewart said, "I think if you would like to try that, you should, but you must promise us that if you start to feel strange again, you'll come back here immediately."

"Okay, I promise."

Mr. Stewart seemed genuinely fond of the idea. "Well, of course he should move back into his room. We can't have expected him to sleep out in that tent for the rest of his life." He looked at David now, stood up, and patted him on the back as he spoke. "I think it's fantastic that you have made so much progress, and if moving outside has been this successful for you, then that has to be acknowledged! It has to mean something."

David sat in uncertain silence at this until Mr. Stewart added, "We have faith in you, son." This was a sentiment that no adult had ever even come close to sharing with David, and the sincerity on the face of both the Stewarts was enough to create a thick lump in David's throat that he had to swallow down before he was able to speak again.

After this, the three of them sat and talked for a few hours, and nothing of any real importance was mentioned. They talked about Mr. Stewart's childhood or people they'd known, and occasionally someone threw in a joke or two.

David felt an entirely new sense of gratitude at having someone older and more mature to whom he could relate. He was appalled at how normal people take for granted the fact that their parents merely care. All that he had ever known was neglect or abuse, and he'd never gotten close enough to any peer who was in a different parental situation to realize what he was really missing.

When David got back inside it was four-thirty. He spent about an hour moving all of his belongings back into his room, all the while avoiding his parents. He came downstairs and saw the trash still sitting by the table, reminding him again that he had forgotten to do what his mother had asked. He rushed over to it and picked it up, hoping that the garbage men were running late today. When he got halfway down the driveway he saw that the garbage truck was picking up his neighbor's trash, so he quickened his pace a little. David and the truck both arrived at the end of his driveway at the same time.

A tall black man stepped off the back of the truck. To avoid the southern, autumn chill, he wore a black jumpsuit with a black hood that shaded out his entire face. David suddenly felt his familiar, wild desire to fight, but it was only then that he realized that his desire had never been to actually *fight*, but to defend himself. His defenses had been heightened around his father, and now he felt as though he needed to defend himself from this man. Most of the man's face was in shadow, and David could see only a few silver teeth in his malicious grin, and his eyes. His eyes were intensely evil. They seemed to have no white in them at all. What should have been white was a faint greenish glow, and the pupils gleamed a faint red shine in the fading sunlight. David mechanically handed the man the garbage bag instead of putting it in the trash can and had to back away, staring silently.

The man took it. "You feel it, dontcha?" the man smiled a horrible, knowing smile. His voice was deep and gruff. It seemed to vibrate, almost as if he had emphysema and had to use a machine to talk.

David did feel it. He didn't know what it was, but he felt it. It was like an invisible sphere around the man, and when David was too close, he felt that strong surge of feelings that he had experienced in the house over a month ago. Those sick desires were trapped inside an invisible orb surrounding this man, and David didn't like it at all. He wanted to get away.

"You just made a huge mistake, moving all of your stuff back into that house," the man croaked conversationally. "They always make a mistake. That's what always ends it for 'em, that one mistake, and moving back into that house, that ended it for you too." He slowly bent closer to David's face and spoke knowingly. "You may as well just end it now; spare yourself, your friends, and your family the suffering. It's gonna come on so hard you won't know what hit you. You won't have a chance to realize what's happened, so you'll end up just like Mr. Batterman—like all the rest." A streetlight flicked on, and David backed away even more. The man kept coming closer to him, and he began to laugh. It was a quiet laugh, but it was horrible; it matched his knowing grin. A chuckle: Uh huh! Ah ha haa! At first it was soft and creepy, and then the last haa became high-pitched and kept sounding aaaaa until it faded into a soft, high-pitched wheeze. He did this over and over until David turned and ran back to his house. He continued to hear that laugh all through the night, and, consequently, he slept very little.

22

David got up in the morning after only an hour or two of sleep and took a shower before breakfast. Now that it was daylight, he could finally shake the haunting image of that demon-eyed garbage man, and after such an exhausting sleepless night, he wondered whether he'd actually seen the man at all. His eyes kept closing and his head kept lolling to the side in the comforting warmth of the shower, but if he let himself fall asleep now, he would probably sleep all day. He'd just have to suck it up until late this afternoon so he didn't completely ruin his sleep schedule.

Trying his best to not think about what the garbage man had said, he walked mechanically down the stairs to pour himself a bowl of stale cereal. His parents were both in and out of the kitchen, but he poured the cereal and sat down to eat anyway, mostly because he was too tired to carry it back upstairs. After a couple minutes of staring at the bowl, David looked up with extremely heavy eyes and saw that his father was glaring at him.

"Why don't you get your worthless ass up and do something productive?" his father sneered.

David might have died. Everything went black. Screw the red haze—his world was completely gone. No longer was he tired or listless or calm; his veins were exploding with adrenaline. In a flash he was up, on top of the counter, and smashing the glass bowl of cereal over his unsuspecting father's head.

"YOU SON OF A—" his father started, bringing his arms up just an instant too late to protect himself, but David was leaping straight up off of the counter, curling his knees in for maximum height, and smashing his feet down onto Pete's head. His father grunted and fell backwards. David grabbed his hair and lifted his head off of the ground a few inches. After repeatedly slamming it back down, he held it up and swung a cabinet open, hitting the front of Pete's face. His eyes went bloodshot and his struggling body went limp, but David continued to pound his father's limp, empty skull sideways against the closed cabinet. Janet rushed in throwing a fit, screaming for him to stop, but he hardly heard a word she said. Then he curled his fists into Pete's bloody clothes, lifted almost his entire body up to his waist, turned toward his mother, and charged at her, hurling the limp body into her gut. Pete collided with her upper half, and they both fell to the floor in a jumbled mass, Pete's girth knocking the wind out of her as she grunted and wheezed.

For one terrifying instant, David's only coherent thoughts were images of his father smiling to himself at regaining the opportunity to harass his son and then of that smugness crashing down around him as that same son smashed the ever-loving shit out of his skull. After this, David felt angry at his oafish father for provoking him again. Didn't he know how much stress David was under?

"Fuck you!" he yelled. "I fucking hate both of you!"

He turned and walked shakily and furiously out of the house, ignoring the thick gore coating the cabinet and linoleum, and the haze evaporated in the intense, sobering sunlight.

Oh, God. What is happening to me?

With nowhere else to go and few other options, he started off to get Megan and Jess.

"Oh, gosh," Megan said when he arrived at her doorstep. "You look awful. What happened?" She glanced behind her uneasily and stepped outside to close the door.

"Yeah, I don't feel too great either." He felt frantic and wasted no time. Squeezing the bridge of his nose and closing his eyes tightly, he said, "Look, last night I saw this guy—this garbage man—and he talked to me. He said that it was a mistake moving back inside, and it would hit me so hard I wouldn't have a clue what was happening."

"What will hit you? David, what are you talking about?"

"I don't know," he said impatiently. He shouldn't have to be wasting all this time trying to make her understand what he was going through. He needed this fixed. "Listen, he wasn't just talking about the curse. He was creepy, like he was trying to scare me or something. Something about him was really . . . off. But he was right: this morning I attacked my parents again. This time there was no warning, no feelings at all before it happened. I just pretty much saw a black haze that disappeared when I walked outside. It's like I almost went blind and my own mind was watching my body through a window or something."

"Well, just move back into the tent." She seemed far too calm, and she clearly didn't understand what David was saying.

"Yes, I definitely will. I have to, but first I want to go tell Jess."

"Don't worry about it. It isn't that big of a deal anyway." She noticed his incredulity and hastily added, "Well, I mean it is, but it can wait. Just tell him next time he comes over."

"Not a big deal?" he asked angrily. "You don't understand! I am cursed! This fucking garbage man was like a part of the house, a part of the curse, and he knew that everything was about to blow up!"

"David, stop freaking out!" she snapped back. "I know it's hard, but we'll get you moved back into the tent, and everything is going to go back to normal, just like it was."

"No it won't," David growled stubbornly. "I fucked it all up by moving back in. Justin fucked everything up for me!"

"Shut up!" she yelled over David's rant. "Just sit down and talk like a normal person. You can't just blame others for it, or you'll never get anything fixed for yourself."

David stood for a moment, shocked by her outburst, then he finally sighed, "Okay," and sat down, rubbing his eyes. "I will then."

Megan sat down beside him and grabbed his shoulder to push his back against her front door. "Listen, David, you have problems at home, and who doesn't? We both know yours are just more extreme, and things like this are bound to happen."

He cut her off. "More extreme? You don't understand! I had no warning!" He lowered his voice, worn out, "It's like I did nothing at all . . . like it wasn't even me."

"That's just in the heat of the moment."

"No. That garbage man knew. The curse is real, and he knows about it. He knew what would happen! I have to talk to him!" He began getting worked up, then sighed and calmed again, "But I couldn't because he was . . . because I'm afraid of him. He was terrible."

"What do you mean? What did he say to you?"

David told her how the man himself had seemed to personify his curse. He told her everything that the man had said to him and how he was utterly terrifying.

"But there isn't a curse, David!"

"There is! I can feel it, and you can too! Everyone can. It's just that no one notices it unless they pay attention. I dreamt of you. I dreamt of all of you, and now the garbage man told me what was going to happen, and it did! He's a part of the curse. None of this is natural! That house let me to see the future, and the garbage man can see it too."

She sat silently for a few moments, apparently hoping that David would realize the lunacy of his assumptions without her help. "No, I don't think that's it," she said finally.

"Well, you don't know. You didn't see my dream, so how can you know about it? I saw you and Shaggy and Mr. Stewart all die. I saw everyone die."

"So you're saying that, because your house is cursed, we're all going to die? Because you saw it in a dream?" Now her disgust was quite obvious.

"No, I didn't mean it like that." David felt reproved.

"Well, that's what you're saying. You're saying that the house is cursed, and now you can predict the future. I'll admit that something is desperately wrong in that house, but I can't say for certain that it has anything to do with the house itself." David felt sorry for his persistence. "It's a lot to think about, and I feel overwhelmed right now." She stood up and opened her door. "Goodbye, David."

"Megan, wait." He stood as well, looking down, ashamed. "I'm sorry."

"Bye." The door closed.

David went back home and walked inside. His mother was still weeping over her unconscious husband, trying to bring him to, but David paid them no attention and walked upstairs to his room with a determined scowl on his face. He began moving things outside to put back into the tent.

Several hours later, as the day's last light was fading in the distance, David walked over to his desk. The light was dim in the tent, and he was very tired, but he could see himself in the small mirror he had placed on top of the desk. What he noticed almost made him scream aloud. The left side of his face was normal, but the right side was in shadow, and what he saw there was a green glow where his eye should be, with a red dot for a pupil. Frantically, he turned around and grabbed his book light. He shined it on his face, but his eyes were normal.

Oh, my God! What was that?

He turned to see if anyone was behind him. No one was there. He walked to the tent's door and spread apart the flaps. No one was outside either, just a shining streetlight and the occasional dog barking in the distance.

He stood extremely still and looked all around his tent with a painfully beating heart. He was sure that what he had seen was that garbage man behind him in the mirror. After a while he calmed down and convinced himself that it was just a trick of the dim light.

He walked to the edge of his mattresses and sat down on the edge. He was about to lie back and go to sleep when he noticed Shaggy sitting uncomfortably in the corner of the tent, staring intently at David.

"Come here, boy," he said in a soft voice with which almost anyone talks to a pet, but Shaggy just turned his head and took a step backwards. "What's wrong, buddy?" David asked quizzically, getting back off the bed and approaching his shaking dog. Shaggy turned around and lay down, ignoring him; David reached down to pet him and pick him up, but he just whimpered stubbornly. "Oh, come on, quit acting stupid. I'm already on edge."

Shaggy lifted his head to look at David untrustingly, and then laid it back down. David stood up and walked over to his desk. He opened a drawer and got a bag of treats that Shaggy simply could not resist. He got one out and walked back over to the dog and held the treat out in his hand.

"Here you go."

Shaggy looked at it for a second. There was something uneasy about him that David didn't like. Shaggy got up and walked to the small bone, picked it up in his mouth, and walked back to the edge of the tent.

David began to get irritated. "Come on, Shaggy, what's your problem? It's just me!"

He finally gave up and lay on his back in his makeshift bed with his arms behind his head. Even Shaggy was being standoffish and unfriendly to David in his time of greatest need.

"Stupid dog . . ." Only now it didn't sound like David's voice. It sounded closer to the dry rumble of a voice that belonged to the garbage man who spoke to David twenty-four hours before.

Shaggy suddenly went berserk. He got up, barking and howling hysterically, ran to the door of the tent, and began jumping up and down and scratching at the canvas side. David nearly jumped out of his skin. He shot up to his feet and turned around, backing away at the same time. He half expected to see the garbage man standing behind him. He tripped over Shaggy's food bowl and landed hard on his backside. His eyes were huge, and he was almost in tears from fear and panic. He kept pushing himself backwards with his feet. When he got to the edge of the tent he got to his hands and knees and crawled into one of the corners. He sat there for a long time with his eyes closed, listening to Shaggy's wails of trepidation.

Shaggy had never acted like this before. He had always been so close to David. He was one of David's only true friends. He would never turn his back on David or hurt his feelings or reject his attention. Why was he acting like this now? Well, the answer wasn't simple, but David knew.

The relevant question was: Why was David acting like this? Was it really only Shaggy, after all this time, who was trying to show him what he couldn't himself admit?

After a while of sitting in the corner of the tent, he stood up. Shaggy was still extremely uneasy at the sight of David. His barks had died down, but he still stayed very far from his owner. David didn't even bother trying to get him to come now; he was much too exhausted, and he was somewhat pissed at Shaggy for putting them both on edge. He walked over to his bed and lay down to finally get some sleep.

23

The time finally came to go back to school. David was glad to be getting away from the house. He was starting to feel odd even while in his tent; he could almost sense a cursed presence emanating outward from the house.

On the bus, David took his usual seat with Jess and sat in an uncomfortable silence for a few moments. After such a harrowing few weeks, David was no longer interested in regaling Jess with his stories and concerns. Jess seemed to know that something wasn't right, as he kept glancing awkwardly at David but saying nothing.

When they were out of the neighborhood and on the long and lonely road that connected the subdivision of Marlboro Hills with the rest of Thriftson County, Jess finally asked David about the last bundle of comics that he had borrowed weeks before.

David sighed. "I'm sorry. There's just been too much going on, and I haven't been able to read them."

Jess nodded and resumed the uncomfortable silence.

Once at school, David went to his locker to get the books for his first class. Closing his locker, he glanced over and saw that some of the usual guys were picking on Jess; they wasted no time. Feeling an overwhelming amount of hatred and anger, he started over to them, but a large hand came down on his shoulder and stopped him in his tracks.

"And just where do we think we're going?" asked a grumbling voice, indulging in its own superior tone.

David turned to see a tall, lanky twelfth grader with a five o'clock shadow and pimples all over his face. He had brown, wavy hair that came halfway down his forehead and a camouflage cap that shouldn't even have been on his head during school. His teeth were brownish-yellow and his gums swollen and black from years of tobacco use. His breath stank tremendously. David was neither surprised nor concerned to recognize him as Justin Guy.

"I'm going to get your apes off of my friend," he sneered back at Justin.

"No, you ain't. Your boyfriend's gonna have to pay the price."

"Pay what price? What did he ever do to you?" David asked indignantly.

"Well, you see, your boyfriend over there, yeah, he's a queer. So we're gonna have to teach him a lesson. Hopefully y'all can learn somethin' from it this time," Justin said with a sarcastically businesslike nod.

David's stomach rolled in embarrassment at having just heard such a ridiculous remark. "Look, jackass—Jess isn't gay, and if he needs a lesson to be taught, it should be not to let bigots like you push him around all the time."

Justin forced a fake laugh and reared back his fist. As it came down, David ducked, and it hit a locker hard enough to dent it.

"Ack!" Justin screamed, pulling his fist away and clutching it in his other hand.

David hurried over to where Jess was being pushed against the lockers and slapped tauntingly in the face several times.

"Come on, retard," a guy with braces and brown hair said. He also wore a camouflage hat. In fact, nearly everyone in Justin's group did, despite the school's policies against hats being worn inside.

"What's wrong, pussy?" another chimed in with a snigger.

"All right, that's enough!" David yelled, slamming his fist into the locker beside Jess's head to create a resounding clang. He took Jess by the arm and started pulling away, but as he turned he saw Justin coming towards him. "Oh, good," David moaned. "Just go, Jess."

"Yeah, just go, pretty boy. We'll deal with you later," Justin sneered as he closed in on David.

But Jess didn't go, he stood by David, and although he didn't say anything in their defense, David was impressed.

"Okay," one of the other guys said to Justin with a grin, "Looks like we're gettin' a two-for-one special."

"Look," David said reasonably, "We never did anything to any of you, so please just leave us alone."

"Aw, the little baby's apologizing," said one of them in a mocking voice.

David flared with annoyance at their false sense of superiority.

"No, I'm not apologizing. We didn't *do* anything," but Justin pushed David against a locker and pushed Jess out of the way. He hauled back his fist and hit David hard in the face. The back of his head slammed into the locker, creating flashing lights behind his closed eyelids.

"Stop!" Jess cried, but everyone ignored him. They all gathered around and cried, "Ohh!" and "Yeah! Get 'im, Justin!"

Maybe Justin would actually kill him this time—put him out of his misery. Perhaps that would be for the best. No more concerns over cursed houses or garbage men or harrowing parents or . . .

David absorbed another sharp blow with a numb, self-loathing acceptance. He thought briefly that it should have hurt more than it did, but by the time he'd been punched three more times, a familiar sharp ache settled rapidly and completely in his head like a drop of dye permeating throughout a clear liquid.

He thought for sure that a teacher would come soon, but no one did. He just stood there, pinned between Justin and the lockers, getting hit over and over in the face. He felt it with excruciating detail when his nose began to bleed, when his upper and lower jaws collided and probably cracked several teeth, every time the back of his head hit the locker, every time Justin's fist slammed into his nose and jaw. He could clearly see through his swollen eyes a fist hurtling at his face at full speed; his vision jarred every time it hit him and every time his head hit the locker. Finally, when the bell rang, the beating stopped and the crowd dispersed. Jess stood a few feet in front of him, staring wide-eyed at David's blood-stained face and shirt.

"Are you okay?" he asked cautiously.

"Yeah, I'm great. Never been better," David said with a surge of impatience running through him. He was angry at the world, even angry at Jess. "Let's go."

"How . . . doesn't that hurt?" Jess asked incredulously.

"Yeah," he said matter-of-factly, "But I guess I'm getting used to it." He was wholly fed up with human interaction.

Once in his first class, David took his seat in the back of the room. His teacher, Mr. Mooring, stood up to begin class. He looked around the room to make sure everyone was there. As he did this, he greeted the class.

"Welcome back. I hope you have all had a great Thanksgiving holiday, because we have a lot of material to cover now that you're back.

First—" he glanced down at a stack of papers on his desk. When he looked back up, his eyes fell upon David, who was sitting at his desk in the corner, helplessly bleeding all over his shirt. "Mr. . . err . . . Mr. Slate, is there a problem?" he asked slowly, seeming confused.

David looked up and pulled his shirt collar away from his nose.

"No, I just have a nosebleed."

"A nosebleed? Your entire face is swollen, David."

"Yes, sir. I fell down."

"You fell down?" he asked, placing a hand on his hip. David could tell he didn't believe him, but he nodded nonetheless. "Well, maybe you should go see the nurse, Mr. Slate," he said, shaking his head in annoyed disbelief.

David got up, still holding his shirt tightly to his nose, and walked out of the classroom. Once in the hall, he turned and headed toward the restroom. The last thing he needed was a school nurse asking him questions about some remorseless senior who would surely put him in the hospital as soon as he got a chance.

David approached the sink and turned on the faucet. He got some paper towels and held them under the flow of water before applying them to his wounds. The water burned when it touched his gums, and the pain throbbed in his nose. With the flares of pain becoming more and more intense, his vision began to blur, and he started to feel light-headed. He swayed to his right and grabbed the sink in an effort to steady himself, but this was no help. He felt as if all of his muscles were deadened with Novocain. His arms just slid limply off the rim of the sink, and he sank to his knees. Suddenly he was aware of nothing. His eyes closed and he slumped against the wall, unconscious.

24

He was at the garbage can again, waiting for someone. Consciously, David was watching himself leaning against the garbage can. This was no ordinary dream. It was as if he were inside a room, watching himself through a window. He had a view that was behind and above himself, as though watching himself from behind.

He could see himself at the garbage can, and he had mixed emotions, but he knew that he wanted revenge. He thought consciously of his previous dream from so many months ago. This profound self-awareness was an odd feeling, especially in a dream. His observing mind knew that he was dreaming, but this in no way affected his mood or determination.

In the last dream he was puzzled about what he was waiting for, but now he knew that he was waiting for the garbage men to come. He understood this now.

As the David on the street stood and waited, the on-looking David remembered the people that would have been behind him, had this been the same dream. It seemed the same; it seemed as though it were just picking up where it left off, but the watcher/thinker knew that this was a completely different dream, over four months later. He tried to get the waiting David to turn to look, but he couldn't.

Come on. Come on, you heartless fucks!

David jumped and spun around. It took him a moment to realize that the voice was in his head. It was his voice. But the onlooking-David wasn't thinking it; the dream-David was thinking it. His mind relaxed, and he turned back to look down the street in the direction from which the garbage truck would come.

Onlooking-David had no physical control over dream-David, but he had mental control. He tried to think of a way to make the dream version of himself turn around to look back down the dark street.

TURN! TURN AND LOOK! DON'T YOU REMEMBER THE PEO-

PLE? THEY'RE YOUR FRIENDS! YOU HAVE TO HELP THEM! TURN AND LOOK!

It was useless. The dream-David just stood, looking back and forth, up and down the street. He looked at his watch.

Any minute now . . .

LOOK! WHAT IS BEHIND YOU?

Then, as the dream-David stood, looking around, he glanced backward and the watcher-David saw that there was nothing, just darkness. It was only the edge of the woods, and he could see nothing because it was unnaturally dark out.

Then, as the onlooking-David's spirits were steadily sinking, he saw the garbage truck coming down the street. It didn't bother stopping at anyone's house, but David knew that it had only one stop on its round today. It slowed to a halt mere inches from dream-David. David could not see his own face, but he knew that he was wearing an intense, determined scowl.

The black, shadowy, hooded figure stepped down from the back of the truck and walked to the garbage can. He placed his hands on the handles and looked, not at dream-David—who stood directly in front of him and whose vengeful, rage-filled mind had been replaced by one filled with a mixture of fear and pity—but at onlooking-David. He consciously tried to look away, but he had no body. He wasn't really there, and he couldn't move or shift his gaze at all; he had no connection with his body that stood at the street below.

The garbage man smiled, staring straight up and into David's own mind, and David saw the silver gleam of his teeth. He could also see the green and red glow of his eyes. His hellish grin slowly spread across his face. David heard the garbage man's dry chuckle, and he could feel him burrowing deeper and deeper into his own subconscious.

Finally, the man looked down at the David that stood directly in front of him.

"I told ya," the garbage man said. "It's hit you hard hasn't it? Well, it ain't over yet, boy. You ain't seen nothin' yet!" His eyes widened comically, and the garbage man produced an elderly, high-pitched chuckle again. "Nope, this ain't even the half of it."

He turned with the garbage can, walked to the truck and dumped it in the back, then walked back to the curb and placed it in its original position.

"I'll be seein' you around, kid," he said with that same merciless grin on his face. Then he turned and walked back to the truck.

"Wait!" the dream-David finally growled as he the garbage man jumped onto the back of the truck. David started toward the truck, suddenly filled with rage, but as he took the first step—

SPLASH!

David jerked, severely needing oxygen, but many hands were holding him down. His head had hit something hard, but his pain was momentarily gone. He was upside down in about six inches of water; he realized he was being drowned in a toilet.

Not just a toilet, he thought, his brain flooding with sympathetic neurotransmitters not for the first time today, but a disgusting, piss-filled, school toilet.

He opened his eyes and shut them hastily as they burned intensely. Urine filled his nostrils and seemed to be attacking his brain. He was getting dizzy, and his head seemed to be on the verge of exploding. There was only blackness until it was overcome by a grayish haze. He groped for something, anything, with his free hands. His right hand hit the toilet paper dispenser and grabbed ahold. He gathered every last ounce of energy that he had, curled one leg up so that his foot was planted firmly on the ground beneath him, and leapt backward, thrusting himself with his leg and arms.

The back of his head slammed into something hard and he heard a deep yelp of pain. With less resistance than anticipated, he slipped as he came upright and landed on his back; he immediately rolled over, retching.

Slowly, David opened his eyes and seemed to be watching himself from afar again, as if still in his dream, but this time he knew that it was real. He saw himself lying on the floor, vomiting, and wallowing in human piss. The room seemed to be filled with a light red haze, and he could hear himself swearing and threatening in his own mind. The real David, who was completely oblivious to his own actions, pushed himself off of the floor and looked out of the stall. He saw that the hard thing his head had hit was actually Justin Guy's nose. Justin sat against the wall clutching his face, eyes wide in disbelief as blood poured through his interlocked fingers.

Once again, David seemed to have no control over himself. He was thinking sanely from behind his window, but he was acting insanely.

Stop. Just walk out and go get a teacher, his mind was insisting. This was a new level of loss-of-control; his conscious mind was completely disconnected.

The physical-David calmly stood up, bent forward, and wrapped his hands around Justin's throat.

25

David had his eyes closed, so he was seeing nothing, but he was still actively listening, both to the clamor in the restroom and to the frantic, unintelligible panic in his own head. He could vaguely feel the cold flesh of Justin's neck at his palms; therefore, his mind was able to deduce exactly what was happening even without sight: David was pressing tightly on Justin's throat and repeatedly slamming his head into the wall.

The physical David felt someone grasp his shoulder and try to pull him back, but his body was holding fast in position. He was not budging from his rhythmic rocking back with Justin's head and then forcing it forward again, repeatedly slamming it against the wall.

"Get off 'im!" he heard someone shout. "Sean, come help me. Now!" the voice hissed.

Then David felt another hand grasp his other shoulder and start to tug along with the first. It was no use; his body wasn't budging. He just kept swearing to himself and strangling Justin, feet sliding wildly on the slick, wet floor.

Finally, a third hand grabbed David's hair and the three managed to get him upright. His eyes opened, but his mind was still dissociated from his body.

Oh god, it's over, he thought helplessly.

"Come on, Justin." Sean, Robbie, and the other baboon were holding David against the stall.

"Get up, man!" one of them pleaded, but Justin just sat there, wide-eyed, clutching his throat and gasping for breath.

David's chest was heaving up and down as he panted for breath to keep his hammering heart oxygenated. His observing mind thought again of the urine dripping down his face and clothes, and the physical David threw up once again. The three jerks let go and jumped back, and David fell to his knees. Again, he closed his eyes and there was nothing but blackness with gray fog overlaying it.

Please, his mind pleaded. *Please, just let it go. Just drop the whole thing now. You can get them back later. It's over; you won. They aren't going to do anything else now. Please!*

Slowly, David opened his eyes. His vision was very blurry and his head was throbbing intensely, but he could see through his own eyes. He could think and act with the same mind.

David was suddenly afraid, kneeling in a puddle of his own puke and blood on the urine-flooded floor of the school restroom, with four twelfth-graders (who probably should have graduated two years ago anyway) crowding around him. He felt abandoned, and he suddenly regretted chasing away his more courageous alter ego.

For a few moments, no one said anything; everyone just looked around at each other, and then David stood up and silently started walking toward the door. He pushed past Robbie and Sean, both of whom seemed to be in utter shock. They were pathetic: completely helpless with their fearless leader, Justin, temporarily out of commission.

The hallway was deserted. Some of the classroom doors were open, and lights shined inside, but others were closed and dark. David looked out the window and saw the sun, still high in the sky. Not directly overhead, but still visible as though it were early evening. He looked at his watch and saw that it was, in fact, nearly thirty minutes past four o'clock. School had ended over an hour ago. He wondered why Mr. Mooring had never said anything about his being gone for so long and why none of his classmates had told his next teachers that he had gone to see the nurse and sent someone looking for him. Surely by third period someone would have suspected something. He also wondered why a janitor hadn't come into the restroom and found him before Justin and his gang had. That could have saved David a whole lot of trouble. Or could it have? A janitor would have asked questions, and he didn't need many questions right now, so he decided not to run through all the possible scenarios.

He didn't want to alert a teacher. If only he had the Stewarts' phone number, he could surely call them for a ride home. He needed to talk to them quite badly anyway. A lot of weird things were happening—fast—just like the garbage man said that they would.

He walked down the hall, around a corner, down a flight of stairs, and into the main hall. There was another restroom here. He walked inside, turned on the sink, and stuck his entire head into the bowl. He closed his eyes and let the cool water run all over his achy head and face. At first water flooded startlingly into his nostrils, but after a few seconds it felt nothing short of divine. He stayed under the faucet for over a full minute before standing upright and getting some paper towels to wipe away the blood and muck.

After washing as much urine out of his hair as possible, David started toward the front door, trying to figure out a way home. It was at least fifteen miles through town and down a lonely, dirt road, winding through the woods. He walked out the door and down the front steps and started across the street on what would surely be a very long, exhausting trip home. No one ever drove on that road except for the people who lived in Marlboro Hills on their way to and from work, the school bus each morning and afternoon . . . and, of course, once a week . . . the garbage men.

26

David hummed to himself as he walked through the town. Alabama seemed to be an old-fashioned state (Thriftson County, at least, seemed it). The buildings were made of weathered bricks and had vines and weeds growing all around them. He passed a liquor store, a movie theater, a pawnshop, a thrift store, and a few random gas stations. Cars were buzzing around, and people were walking up and down the sidewalks. Several people stared untrustingly at David, as he had not managed to clean himself very well in the restroom sink; his hair was greasy and matted, his nose was red and swollen, and he had bruises and small scrapes all over his face.

No one actually interrogated him or even asked if he needed any help, despite his appearance. He thought this was for the better, as he had no idea what was happening to him. When he took time to recall how disassociated he had felt in that restroom brawl, he became very concerned for his mental well-being. For this reason he thought it best to suck it up and make the several-mile hike home without stopping a stranger and asking for a ride, but it had only been four miles and just over an hour, and already David was ready to collapse.

Just before six, he sat down on a bench outside an auto-body shop. A lot of cars were going the way that he was headed because many of the middle-class suburban jobs ended around five or six o'clock. Despite his exhaustion, David was still too fearful to ask someone for help. Not only was he worried about hurting someone, he was worried about having to explain himself to a complete stranger on a ten-minute car ride.

The sun was quickly going down, and David was finding that fewer and fewer vehicles were passing in his direction. It was half past six o'clock now, and he was just about to the outskirts of the dark, lonely woodland that lay ahead. He was thankful for the cool autumnal evening temperature, but he was still exhausted from physical exertion and stress. He even thought about simply stopping somewhere for the night and sleeping on the ground. His parents would never miss him, but the thought of spending all night in the woods made him feel more uneasy than ever. He finally decided to stop and rest for ten or fifteen minutes before continuing on down the ten-mile road that led him through the vast woodlands and into Marlboro Hills.

He finally stepped onto the dirt road that led through the woodland at ten minutes before seven o'clock. The sun was now almost completely gone; the moon was visible through the trees, and small slivers of moonlight shone onto the ground through the leaves, creating various shapes and outlines, some small and others larger. The shapes of light slithered and swayed as the trees rocked gently in the breeze, and the shimmery movement of the dim light made David feel as though he were in a dream, walking at the bottom of a pool of dark water.

The dirt road was pretty straight, but it had a few small curves, which, combined with the distance, made his neighborhood impossible to see. Thirty minutes into the walk, the town had completely disappeared behind him, along with the sun. Cars had stopped coming by, and, not for the first time, David felt as though he were going to pass out. His head was still swimming and achy after his two run-ins with Justin earlier today.

After another thirty minutes, the world began to spin and shift. His night-vision was worsening—either that or the night was growing steadily darker—and he began losing his balance. He had to sit down. He estimated that he was only about two or three miles into the ten-mile journey that lay ahead, as his pacing was slowing considerably. It was eight o'clock, and he thought he was going about one mile every twenty-five minutes, which meant that with about eight miles to go, it would take him at least three more hours to get back home.

Eleven o'clock, three whole hours of walking: this was going to be a very long night.

27

By nine o'clock, it was completely dark; David couldn't even see the moon anymore, as all of the trees had grown steadily more dense. He had seen only two cars passing in the past hour, and neither of them gave any indication that the drivers considered slowing down or stopping. He thought that he must be at least four miles into the forest, and he had long since contemplated turning back and staying in the town for the night. Missing one day of school wouldn't be so bad, especially under the current circumstances, but it was much too late now for turning back. He knew that he must be nearly halfway home but that he would never make it. His pace was slowing exponentially, and he was too tired to even think straight: not good in his current state. He would likely have to spend the night alone in the dark forest.

Yet again, David stopped to sit down and allow his body to rest for a few moments. He had a tremendous stitch in his side and was beginning to feel a cramp in his left calf. Sitting alone in the dark, quiet forest, he took off his shoes to flex his toes and spread them apart. They cracked and popped willingly on both feet, and David stretched each leg out one at a time and slowly pulled them back inward, stretching his quadriceps muscles.

Once his legs began feeling marginally better, David allowed his body to relax wholly, and he just sat looking around into the darkness. Every time he thought that he could stand to get comfortable in the grass and just go to sleep until morning, he heard an unsettling noise. He sat and listened for three or four minutes to the sleepy sound of countless bugs chirruping all around him. Against their chorus, the sporadic cry of a rodent or bird or, occasionally, something larger, sounded decisively out-of-place and threatening.

He finally decided that he had absolutely no desire to stop moving and become easy prey for God-only-knew-what out in this remote forest. He stood up, looked sleepily in the direction that he was heading, thought momentarily of how horrid it would be if he somehow lost his direction and began heading back the other way toward town, and took a single step forward. Suddenly a brilliant light shone onto him from about twenty feet into the woods on his left.

The light completely blinded David after he had become so accustomed to the complete darkness for over two hours. Everything became a white glow, and nothing was visible for almost thirty seconds. Soon David began to see vague silhouettes of trees pop back into focus. He put a hand up to shield his eyes and looked into the woods. For a few seconds, he saw only a large, glowing ball, but then it slowly became clearer and split in two. The two bright balls spread apart and their light seemed less intense. David saw two lights side-by-side. Behind the lights, a large vehicle slowly came into focus. After about a minute of his eyes adjusting, David finally saw the familiar white garbage truck with the headlights on, sitting in a small clearing a short distance through the thick trees.

Suddenly there was a click and a rumble as the truck's engine ignited, and it revved and began lurching forward. David called out, turned, and ran as fast as he could in the direction that he thought he had been heading before.

The truck screamed out of the trees behind David, somehow weaving through a seemingly nonexistent trail, and sped after him. As it came to almost a foot behind him, David hurled himself out of the road and onto the ground at the trees' edge. He saw the black man in the plain black jumpsuit, standing on the back and holding the safety pole on the truck as he rushed by. The man's head turned to David as the truck passed, and he saw two green eyes with sinister red glowing pupils. He saw them for only a split second, and then the truck skidded and spun halfway around, sending dirt and gravel flying. It came to a halt, blocking the entire roadway.

David looked into the windshield and saw two more green glows with red pupils. Then he heard the crunch of gravel and a rough, haggard voice call, "Ay! Lights!" The headlights quickly faded out, and David was once again momentarily blinded by the encompassing darkness.

Slowly, a tall, hooded silhouette came into view beside the truck. The garbage man's eyes shone, but now, in the darkness, his teeth did not gleam.

"I told ya you were done for, David. I warned you," a dry voice said as the figure slowly stepped forward. The amount of time between each slow crunching footstep added just the right amount of mysterious evil to the man's voice and threats.

David stood up, fearing for his life like never before. "You didn't warn me anything!"

"Yes, I warned you," the man croaked simply. David could tell that the man was enjoying every second of his sadistic torment.

"NO! You only told me that it would hit me hard now that I moved back in, so I moved back out. I moved out the very next day!" His heart was frantically beating against his sternum like a trapped bird, and he was nearly pleading with the garbage man, as though he were the cause of all of David's woes. He could still hear the crunch of gravel with every step the man took. "You have no idea what's going on with me. Why are you following me?" he demanded.

"You will soon be finished, David. Do you hear me? Finished!" The garbage man suddenly sounded angry, which made his presence even more foreboding.

But David persisted nonetheless. "What do you mean, finished? Who are you? What do you want from me?"

"Don't you know? Haven't you figured that out yet? I thought you were smart enough to get it by now. I *know* you're smart enough. You've known us all along, David. You're just too distracted to do anything about it," he said angrily.

"DISTRACTED?" David demanded, anger rapidly replacing his desperate fear. "I'll say! What is happening to me? I know that you have something to do with it!" He was suddenly prepared to beat an explanation out of this creep. He could feel his mind pulling itself away from his body yet again.

Though the garbage man laughed his wicked laugh, he scowled, obviously feeling as defensive and offended as David. "Somethin' to do with it? I *am* it, you foolish scab, and if you don't acknowledge that soon, I'm gonna bring ya whole fucking world down around ya ears, David." He paused. "How's that little girlie I see you with so much?"

"Don't," David said, closing his eyes and trying to remain in control. He knew that getting physical with this guy could mean rapid death for himself, but still he struggled to remain calm.

"Megan, right?" the man chuckled tauntingly. "Yeah, that's right. I sure wouldn't mind giving her a visit right now."

"Leave her out of it!" he screamed, fists clinching and legs shaking, filled with adrenaline.

"Yeah, you know what I mean," he said sadistically.

David finally lunged at the man and leaned forward to tackle him at the waist, but at the last second, the garbage man stepped carelessly aside. David fell flat on his chest, taking his breath away and scraping his chest through his shirt.

The garbage man chuckled uproariously as David groaned and writhed on the ground. "I'll see you around, David," he said through fits of sadistic laughter.

He turned, walked, and jumped back onto the garbage truck. He slammed his fist a single time against the side of the truck, and the lights immediately came back on. The engine roared to life, and the truck drove away.

David lay on the ground struggling to catch his breath and calm his nerves, and after a few moments, he no longer felt the indescribable tugging of his mind against itself.

When the truck was finally out of view, everything was again completely black, save for the bright spots of light darting through David's field of vision.

28

After wandering in the woods and contemplating his encounter for a very long time, David decided to stop for the night. He knew that it was after midnight and that he was getting nowhere.

In his exhausted, horrified stupor, he had decided that it was a better idea to leave the slightly curving road and enter the woods. He had figured that, without having to go through all of the curves on the road, the journey would be much quicker. Now he knew that he had been miserably mistaken. He was lost in woods about which he knew nothing, and his legs simply would no longer support him at all. He was so exhausted he felt as though the positive end of a magnet were in his eyelids and the negative end embedded in his cheekbones.

David sat down against a large oak tree, closing his eyes and fighting the urge to cry. He was deeply stressed about the mysterious garbage men. Now he had lost all sense of direction and had no idea how he was going to sleep or what he was going to do in the morning. Cutting straight through the woods had seemed like a good idea, but after about an hour of dodging trees, David got completely disoriented and lost all track of anything and everything. Now he was lost God-only-knew how deep in the woods, at God-only-knew what time of night. He could not have even begun to guess when the sun would rise again. He vaguely feared that it might never.

Now he decided that, if he went to sleep, he could find the road in the sunlight when he woke in the morning. He closed his eyes and thought nostalgically of his old house. He thought about his eventful first day back at school after the holidays. He tried to decide what he wouldn't give simply to be able to move back into his old house, where there was no curse and, more importantly, no garbage men.

29

David was walking through a path. All that he could see was the edge of the trees; the rest was black. The sky was black, the ground was black, and everything in the distance was black. The only things with color were the trees on the edge of the path: a dark, monotonous haze of brown and green.

David continued walking along the path until he came to his own home. His parents were dead, lying on the ground in a mangled heap. Shaggy was close by, also dead. David felt a distant sense of heartache, blocked out by his determination. He turned around and saw Mr. and Mrs. Stewart awkwardly slouched in their armchairs in the street; Mrs. Stewart had her back turned to him and seemed to be brooding over her husband. The image was ghastly and haunting.

David would have stopped, but he was very busy. He was looking for something, something that could be very important.

So he continued walking. He walked for what seemed like an eternity before he saw Jess running away from what appeared to be the unmoving body of Megan on the ground. David's heart seemed to implode inside his chest, and he started to run toward them. What had happened? What had Jess done? David almost started crying; he feared the absolute worst. He took one giant quickstep and started to run, then realized that there were more important matters still at hand. His emotion evaporated as soon as the thought occurred.

What could be more important than his only friend and his only girlfriend ever?

She is gone. Both of them are gone for good, and there is nothing that you can do.

Suddenly realizing that something important was very close, he spun around on his heel, but before he could see anything, his face was poked by a series of very fine, very sharp objects, and everything went black.

30

David came down to his knees hard. He heard the crunch of leaves when he hit. He scratched frantically at his face because whatever had poked it made it tickle and itch terribly. He opened his eyes and looked around, but could see nothing.

He leaned back on the ground and stared up at the sky; several clouds were blocking the light of the moon, and he could see nothing there, either.

How long had he been asleep?

What had poked him?

Suddenly, he sat bolt upright.

"Who's there?" he demanded.

Nothing.

"I said, who's there!" he screamed now, still feeling the vivid tingle on his skin where someone had clearly prodded him.

Silence.

David stood up, heart hammering wildly in his chest. He turned in the opposite direction and ran. He blindly ran as fast as he could, but after just a few steps, his shoulder slammed into the trunk of a tree. He spun and fell onto his back, once again staring at the star-less, moon-less sky, breathing hard.

David lay motionless and listened intently. All around him he could hear the deafening clamor of innumerable insects communicating, fighting, mating, hunting, crawling, flying, and running . . . living. He heard two owls conversing in the distance. The sound made him feel awfully alone. He heard the scurrying of feet in the distance, leaves crunching, all of the natural sounds of a forest, but nothing was too close.

After several nauseating minutes, he decided that it was safe, and he began to doze again. He was almost asleep when a chilling and terribly lonesome sound echoed throughout the night. It was very loud and far too close.

David jumped to his feet and scrambled backwards away from the sound, eyes darting blindly in their sockets, until he hit his back on a tree. There he slumped down and sat, leaning against the tree, not daring to move even his head. The leaves rustled as something slinked toward him. He knew that it wasn't a human because of the frequency of the footfalls. He guessed that it must have at least four legs, maybe more. A high-pitched groan escaped him as he envisioned two black men in dark, hooded jumpsuits slowly approaching, their green and red eyes somehow illuminating their path in the darkness.

The leaves kept cracking closer and closer until David saw two faintly green eyes glowing.

"No," he groaned in a low voice. "Please don't kill me," he pleaded helplessly.

Tears of horror streamed from his stinging eyes as he sat watching for the next pair of green eyes to appear from behind, but then he realized that the eyes were much too low to belong to an approaching garbage man; they were almost eye-level with himself, and he was sitting, leaning against the tree.

Everything around him was completely black, and the eyes were now less than five feet from David's own. His heart was thumping so hard in his chest that it made his throat hurt. His vision jarred with every beat. He could taste the acrid adrenaline in the back of his tongue, which was stuck to the roof of his dry, papery mouth. His breathing was sharp, hurried, and hushed.

The eyes stopped coming closer, and the leaves stopped crunching. A low rumble rose from the hellish interior of whatever stood before him. It grew louder and louder until David recognized it as a beastly growl. His heart began beating so fiercely that he stopped hearing the growl over the drumming of his own organs. He could hear nothing at all except an intense, paralyzed ringing in his head. He closed his eyes, sobbing, begging to himself, "No, no, no. Please, no." His head was shaking so violently that it was practically banging against the tree. His teeth were clanking together so hard that they were in danger of chipping.

When he opened his eyes, he saw the glowing eyes move closer, slowly and almost impossible to notice. They continued drawing near until David saw the silhouette of a coyote's head with razor sharp teeth bared. David shot up to his feet, his entire body breaking out in breathtaking chills. He sobbed loudly, frantically clinging to the tree behind him. The coyote quickly jumped back at David's sudden movement, and it eventually turned and trotted away, snarling and barking. David was deafened from the cocktail of hormones coursing through his bloodstream. He got dizzy and closed his eyes. Finally, he slumped back down and passed out from sheer horror.

31

Slowly, the world faded into view. David could hear birds twittering and squirrels chattering. He saw obscured sunlight filtering through the canopy of the trees. He was suddenly filled with the same fear from the previous night and jumped up to his feet, eyes bulging. He looked around frantically and, seeing that nothing was there, began to gradually calm down.

When he turned around, the thing standing before him induced a dizzying combination of fear and confusion. He begged his eyes to admit deceit. What he had been leaning against, what he had thought was the branchless trunk of an oak tree, was actually the bare side of a pine tree. All of the bark was stripped from this one side from the ground up to about six feet. On the other side, branches protruded as low as two feet from the ground.

David walked around to the other side to get a better look. He felt the tingling of pine needles sticking in his cheek. He remembered last night and realized that the pine needles were what had awakened him before he saw the coyote. He remembered thinking that something important was right beside him in the dream, and this certainly seemed important.

He recalled Mr. Stewart's story: *They mention something about the ground beside the bare side of a pine tree . . .*

David walked back around to the bare side and looked at the ground. It looked the same as any other ground. He bent over and started to move leaves, rocks, and dirt aside. After a few minutes, he began to dig frantically, desperate to find something.

After about twenty minutes of digging, David had a three-cubic-foot hole dug. Out of breath, he gave up and decided to try to find his way home. He spit in his hands and rubbed them together in a vain attempt to clean them. It didn't work too well, so he just wiped them on his pants. He started on his way, feeling more afraid and confused than ever. He had never believed in the existence of the curse as strongly as he did now, after such a God-awful night in these woods.

David looked at his watch and saw that it was eight-thirty. It wasn't exactly the brightest of mornings; the sky was covered with dark, heavy clouds, and he could barely hear the low rumble of thunder far away.

He wondered if it would be too terrible a tragedy if he never did find his way home. Maybe life would be better here in the woods with no house, no parents, and no bullies. But then he remembered the crippling fear from last night and thought that he wouldn't last half a week out here. Plus, there was no food. This was a bad thing to think, because he immediately realized that he was painfully hungry. If he didn't get home soon, he would have to resort to eating . . . something out here.

So David trekked on, thinking of the tree and of what Mr. Stewart had told him so many weeks ago. None of it made any sense. The victims of the house went crazy and killed everyone close to them. Then, when the police found them coming out of the woods, they were muttering something about the bare side of a pine tree, a tree no one else sees or knows about. It just didn't make sense. How could no one notice a pine tree in these woods except the occupants of that house? And now that he had found it, David wondered what had been so special about the ground beside it.

32

As noon approached, David still had no sign of the road or of a neighborhood. For all he knew he could have gotten turned around and was heading back toward the town.

The sky was a dull gray, almost black, which made David's entire surroundings seem gray. It gave him an eerie feeling. Something bad seemed inevitable—or, something *else* bad. There was also a light mist, making the world around him look foggy and desolate.

He finally found the road again after midday. He had stopped to rest a few times, but he still felt as though he would collapse at any second. He couldn't remember being this tired in his entire life, and, to top it off, his stomach was a pulsating knot that felt tighter than his shoelaces.

After two lonely hours of walking on the dirt road with no sign of a vehicle, he stepped into the outer limits of his neighborhood. As he did this, he saw a car coming around the corner on its way home. While walking home through Marlboro Hills he saw five or six more.

When David turned the corner and saw his yard with a big green tent in it, he was so happy that he could have done a back flip, had his legs not felt like rubber. He stumbled all the way down the street and into his front door. He went inside and washed the grime from his hands and arms, drained four glasses of water in a row, then went to the refrigerator and got what he needed to make three turkey sandwiches. After piling extra helpings of cheese and meat onto six pieces of bread, he went to the cabinets and got a bag of stale chips. Finally, he got another glass of water and went back outside. His parents never even noticed.

After he had finished two of his sandwiches and half of the chips, he folded the bag down and put it on his desk. He took his last sandwich and started across the street to the Stewarts' house.

33

When Mrs. Stewart opened the door, her eyes seemed to actually bulge out of her head.

"What on earth happened to you?" she asked frantically.

David didn't understand what she was talking about. He looked down at his stomach in reflex, then at each arm.

"What?" he asked.

"Your face! What in the world did they do to you?"

David had already forgotten about getting beaten up at school. His face just seemed to stop hurting in all the later chaos. He reached up and touched his nose. It was swollen over twice its size and now pain seared through his whole head. He winced and drew his hand quickly away.

"Oh yeah, a guy at school—err—he beat me up. It's no big deal, though, I'm fine."

"No big deal? Wha—why?" She seemed to be at a loss for words to help rationalize why someone would do this to someone like David. He knew how she felt.

She stammered and seemed to lose track of everything she had said. After a brief pause, she said, "And you reek."

He self-consciously wished that he had taken a shower before coming, but too much had happened to wait another ten minutes before talking to Mr. Stewart. "Yeah, I know, they tried to . . . drown me in a toilet, but that was yesterday."

"They tried to drown you?" she asked hysterically. "You have to do something about this nonsense!"

"No, I think they were playing around. I mean, they didn't really want to kill me."

"This isn't a game. You must tell someone."

"No, don't you see? That's the problem. I can't."

"Why can't you?" she asked incredulously.

"Because I—" he thought for a moment and shook his head doubt-fully, "I don't even know what I did. Look, that's not the point; it's not why I'm here . . . not exactly, I mean."

"David, what are you talking about?" she looked more and more worried by the second. "Come in and sit down. You can tell me all about it."

They walked through the kitchen and into the living room, and she asked if he would like anything to eat or drink. He declined, saying that he had just eaten.

Once in the living room, they sat down on the couch, and Mrs. Stewart stared, her lips taut. David looked around feeling self-conscious.

"Where's Mr. Stewart?" he asked. He felt rather awkward without Mr. Stewart, his only prominent father figure.

"Oh, he went into town just a few minutes ago. Just tell me what's happened and I'll let him know."

David took a deep breath and started at the beginning, which was when the garbage men had come. He told her about their warning and about how he had moved back into the tent. He explained how he had actually picked his fat father's unconscious body up off the ground, just to give her an example of the superhuman strength that he seemed to have at times. He explained how he had dreamt that he was watching himself as though through a window, and how, afterwards, he actually seemed to be doing just that in the middle of the day, while he was conscious yet disconnected. He told her how he had no control over his body, but that he thought that he might be able to fool his mind, if he could figure out how. He told her about the bathroom incident and the lengthy walk home, the horrifying night he spent in the woods, and the pine tree that he found when he awoke.

When he finished, Mrs. Stewart was crying silently. She was star-ing at the floor absentmindedly. She gulped and looked solemnly up at him.

"So you are getting these feelings . . . even when you are away from the house?"

"Yes, but only when I get extremely upset or something like that. Usually, only when Justin prompts me."

They sat there for a long while, David growing increasingly fright-ened at Mrs. Stewart's reaction. After a few minutes she told him that she didn't know what else to say.

"Maybe my husband will know what to do, but this sounds like . . . " she paused, reluctant to be so frank, "Like all of the other times." She broke into choking sobs and put her hands over her face. "Oh, this is just awful!"

David didn't know what to do, so he patted her shoulder awkwardly and assured her that he would think of something.

When Mr. Stewart got home, he had the same reaction, only without so many tears. Respectable men like Mr. Stewart rarely cry out. The only advice he could give David sounded futile, repetitive, and seemingly metaphorical: to try extremely hard to communicate with the separate part of his mind and try to convince his body to stop. He was disappointed at their frail attempts to help him overcome this, and reproachful due to their childish creativity when attempting to explain his "condition." He had come over for guidance and ended up patting them on the backs and assuring them that everything would be fine, that he was not like the rest. He left their house at dusk knowing about as much as he had known when he first got there. If his closest confidants were losing their confidence in him, how could he have confidence in himself?

He couldn't help noticing the way that the Stewarts looked at each other when he told Mr. Stewart about the garbage men. It almost seemed that they were ashamed of him, but he refrained from interrogating them about it. If they thought he was hallucinating on top of everything else, he didn't need to know it right away.

What he didn't notice was that, after he walked out the door, Mrs. Stewart shook her head, continued crying, and said to Mr. Stewart:

"There's nothing we can do about it now. He said there were . . . " the last two words were almost a question, "Garbage men?"

As she reached for the phone, Mr. Stewart put his hand on her shoulder and said, "Just give him a few days. Maybe we've misunderstood the boy."

They both sighed and held each other until they fell asleep.

34

After David finally took a very long, very much-needed shower, he went outside to his tent, sat at his desk, and tried to figure out a number of things: Who were these garbage men? What could have possibly been beneath that pine tree? How was it possible for this house to have a curse? How was it possible for him to sometimes lose complete control over his body?

His mind was buzzing with all of these unanswered and seemingly unanswerable questions.

"You woke up next to a pine tree?" Mr. Stewart had asked just under an hour before.

"Yeah. I noticed it as soon as it was daylight."

"So you walked to it in your sleep? Or did you just not notice it as you fell asleep?"

"Well," David had considered the possibility that he just didn't notice the pine in the dark, "I guess I may have been there all along. It was pretty dark."

"But you must have walked some, right?" Mr. Stewart had asked. "You brushed the needles that woke you up, no?"

"Yeah, that's true."

"So, can you lead us back to this tree?" he had asked excitedly.

David suddenly wished that he had paid more attention to how he had gotten back home from that tree, but the woods all seemed to blur. That hellish night had already seemed like a nightmare from another life. "No," he'd admitted, "I didn't think to take notice of where I was."

In the same fashion as when David had mentioned the garbage men, Mr. Stewart averted his eyes uncomfortably, glanced at his wife, and lapsed into a momentary silence as he stared helplessly at the floor.

As David recalled this conversation and struggled to prioritize his innumerable problems, he heard Megan and Jess approaching his driveway. After talking to the Stewarts, David was no longer eager to tell either of them about what had happened to him. He was quickly losing hope, and he knew the people he loved were, as well. He wondered just how much more of his personal problems Megan and Jess would stick around to put up with.

"What happened? Jess says you weren't at school today and that you got into a fight yesterday!" Megan demanded immediately upon entering the tent.

"I'm fine," David said hurriedly, if not a bit defensively. "I fell asleep in the restroom and had to walk home last night." He cocked his head forward and spread his arms as if to say, "What are ya gonna do?"

"Everything's okay," he concluded lamely.

"No, everything is not okay," Megan shot back sternly. "What's going on with you, David? We're terrified."

"Wait," Jess interjected, "You walked all the way home? From the school?"

David just shrugged, and Megan said, "What is it with you, David? Why are you pushing us away, all of a sudden? We're the only people in the world who care about you."

David started to get angry. The last time they talked, Megan had acted like a jerk and completely rejected David's concerns and ideas. "Nothing's going on!" he shouted. "In fact, I think that I'm starting to feel better already." He didn't feel like talking about it anymore today. "And what do you know about who cares about me?" he asked angrily. "You don't know as much about me as you think you do!"

Megan looked reproved. "David," she said softly, "I'm sorry. I didn't mean it like that."

"Look, just . . . go. I'm not feeling well, and I want to go to sleep. I'll see you both later." He closed his eyes and rubbed them distractedly.

Jess, who had said little since they arrived, looked as though he would cry, and Megan squinted her eyes in disgust.

"I love you, David," she said with a terrible, hurt look in her eyes. It was the first time she had ever said it in front of Jess and the last time she ever said it in the present tense.

"I know. I'll see you later," David said, and they left.

He zipped his makeshift door the second they were out of the way, then went and sat down on his sleeping bag. After a few moments, Shaggy began to whine and scratch on the side of the tent to indicate that he wanted to go outside, so David unzipped the door again and coaxed him outside. While Shaggy wandered away, David sat back down on his pallet, and, a few moments later, he heard Jess's voice.

"David?" he must have somehow ditched Megan and come back to try again. What was the use? Why did he think he'd be able to help?

David didn't respond. He just sat staring at his feet as Jess peeked his head into the tent.

"I'm sorry about all this, man. I know it's hard on you," he said simply. "Megan knows it, too. She just wants the old you back. That's all."

"God, Jess," David replied irritably, "This *is* me. There is no old me. This is my goddamn life now, and there's nothing either of you can do about it."

Jess stood in obedient silence for a few moments before saying, "If Superman were real, I bet he'd help us. He wouldn't give up."

David stood up, snatched Jess's comics off his desk, and thrust them angrily into Jess's hands, shouting, "Now's not the time for your fucking comic book bullshit! Just go home, Jess!"

Jess turned dejectedly, shunned and shamed by his only friend, and walked back toward his house. David stomped back to his sleeping bag and sat down.

After several minutes Shaggy returned with a small stick and put it between David's feet.

"Oh, now you want to play? After your little episode the other day?" David became even more irritated and resentful. He picked up the twig, broke it, and threw it into the corner of the tent. Shaggy put his tail between his legs and sat down, staring at David's feet, not quite bold enough to look him in the eye.

"What are you looking at?" David demanded harshly, "Christ. Go lie down!" Shaggy lay down and crawled closer to David, who closed his eyes and began to see red spots.

"Quit! Get out of here! I'm sick of all this shit! I just want to be alone!" David stood up with clenched fists and yelled incomprehensibly through his gritted teeth. Shaggy turned and gravely crept away. David shook his head in disgust, lay down, rolled over, and fell asleep within seconds.

When he awoke the next morning, he rolled over and let his eyes slowly adjust to the sunlight beaming through the pores in his tent. His brain filled immediately with thoughts of everything that had happened during the past few harrowing days, and the calmness that he felt just after waking quickly disappeared. Lying immobile under his sheets with still-heavy eyes, he felt horrible about getting so irritated with his friends and began to plan his apologies. First, he needed to apologize to Shaggy, who had done nothing whatsoever to provoke such an irrational tantrum as David had thrown the night before. He looked at his watch and was startled to find that he had slept over fourteen hours. His legs and arms were tingling; he figured that he moved around very little in the night and must have slept like a rock.

He looked at Shaggy's little bed and saw that it was empty.

"Shaggy?" he asked the silent tent in a groggy voice that was still stiff from the extended hours of slumber. There was no response of a rustling tail or feet, and David hoped that Shaggy wouldn't be too resentful or afraid of him now.

He looked around the tent for the first time and saw with dizzying shock that Shaggy was lying at the edge of the tent in a small puddle of blood. David jumped up in a frantic state of extreme grief and shock and came down to his knees beside Shaggy, tears forming in his burning eyes.

There was a streak of blood about two feet long from where the wounded dog appeared to have tried to crawl. His skull was crushed and his eyes were closed. David began to wail pleadingly. Shaggy, David's closest companion, with whom he had spent every waking hour outside of school for the past three months, was now lying in a pool of blood at the edge of David's tent, which was in this detested yard of a cursed house in a forsaken neighborhood of the insufferable county of Thriftson in the pathetic state of Alabama. His grief quickly turned to anger, and his anger increased with each passing moment. Yet it did not induce any violent outbursts. He felt far too tired to do anything so energetic.

When the shock passed and the reality of the whole situation dawned on David, he quieted his sobs and lay near Shaggy's unmoving body, weeping silently. He cursed himself for his ridiculous behavior the night before, and he wished more than anything that his last interactions with Shaggy, an ever-faithful and trustworthy friend, hadn't been so negative and strained. Before he even wondered how this had happened, he thought how terrible Shaggy must have felt last night with David yelling at him and then going straight to bed. He wished Megan were there; he wanted to hold her in his arms to share his grief.

Afterward, with tears still streaming down his face, he got some paper towels, wrapped Shaggy inside like a mummy, and buried him in the only soft place that he could find—beside a bush near his front porch. All the while, he felt more and more ashamed at defiling the dead body of such a beloved friend. Shaggy deserved better than to be buried in this unstable ground in a situation such as this, but David had nowhere else to go and nothing else to use. The thought of telling Mr. and Mrs. Stewart and asking for their help made him feel nauseous.

Later, he walked to Megan's house and asked her to walk with him. He was in tears as he told her about how he had become angry with Shaggy—just as he had with her and Jess—just before passing out from all his stress. He explained how someone must have snuck into his tent in the middle of the night and crushed poor Shaggy's skull, and how he had pathetically tried to crawl toward David but had made it only a few inches. With each word, his voice became more and more shaky until he finally broke down and cried openly.

Megan put her arm around him, but she seemed aloof. "I'm so sorry."

"I know it was Justin. The bastard. Why would he do this to me?"

"Come on, David. You don't know that. How could you know such a thing?"

"Who else would do that?" he demanded, angry again at her disbelief. "He saw me with Shaggy the other night when he came into my yard and kicked my ass. He's obviously pissed that I returned the favor the other day. It's too much of a coincidence!"

"I know how it looks, David, but you should think twice before you start pointing fingers at someone for something that serious."

"I know he did it! No one else would be that cold," he shouted. "I'm sick of you acting like you don't care, like you don't believe me! And while we're on the subject, the stupid curse is real! There are garbage men, and they are tormenting me, just like Justin is, just like this stupid house is. You can deny it all you want, but I saw the pine tree. I know this is really happening."

Megan sighed and closed her eyes. "Look, I'm stressed out, okay? I'm sick of everything always being the complete worst. I'm really sorry, David, but I can't do this. I can't even talk to you anymore when you're this way." And with that she turned and left him, and she never looked back.

David stood in silent disbelief. He was too angry to be sad about it yet, so he stared after her with a look of disgust as she made her way back into her house. Her front door slammed with a finality that made David's gut wrench. He had a million things he wanted to say and do, but he couldn't think of even one. He turned mechanically and walked back home

When he got back to his tent, he made absolutely no effort to stop himself from smashing, tearing, kicking, and throwing every item that he could find. It seemed even his mind had no objections to this fit.

After his tantrum he sat down lifelessly on his floor and sobbed into his arms until he was hoarse and sleepy. Not because his cheap desk was broken, now standing lopsided on three legs with a shattered drawer beneath it, not because all his favorite books lay in shreds around the tent, and not even because he feared that Justin might slash his way through the tent wall and slit his throat at any moment while he slept. He cried because he had found a feeling unlike any that he had ever experienced, and the world had ripped that feeling—and the loved ones associated with it—away from him just as rapidly as the garbage man had said that it would.

The next morning, after seemingly endless hours of brooding, David looked up from his bed to see Jess standing wordlessly at the edge of his tent. They both knew that David had no desire to wake up and go to school. Jess was obviously stopping by before the bus picked him up. He looked even more grave than David felt. He was holding a newspaper, which he silently held out to David.

The headline read, "Thriftson County High School Student Brutally Murdered."

35

David couldn't decide whether he should be happy or afraid of the sudden brutal murder of Sean Doyle, one of Justin's trusted side-kicks. He definitely wanted to know the specifics. He found it odd that, in light of all the recent events, such an untimely thing could happen, especially while he was contemplating a plan of vengeance upon Justin.

It appeared that Megan was also skeptical about the situation, but she was obviously not as calm about it as David.

"David, what have you done?" she screamed later that afternoon as she stormed into his tent.

"I didn't do that!" David yelled back, his mind startled out of its faraway meditation.

"I mean, I know you were angry with Justin because you think that he had something to do with killing Shaggy, but I didn't think you would actually go this far. This is insane! What are you going to do? How did you expect to get away with something like this?" She was in hysterics. "I can't even believe that I am talking to you right now! We will never be the same after this!"

"Megan, listen to me!" he demanded, standing up from his bed. "I did not do anything to Sean! Last night, after we finished talking and it got dark, I came straight here and went to sleep. This morning I did nothing. I just sat here and waited all day while you were at school."

"I don't know if I can believe you anymore, David."

"Well, at least try," he sneered defensively. "I swear I didn't do it. You know I wouldn't do that! I can't believe you'd actually let that thought enter your head."

"I don't know anything about you anymore."

Just then Jess, who had been standing mildly behind Megan, chimed in, "It's all over the school. Justin told everyone about how you almost killed him in the restroom. Everybody thinks you did it. There are tons of different stories. If you came to school now, you'd probably be lynched."

"Or arrested," Megan quickly added patronizingly.

"I know!" he snapped, looking specifically at Megan. "Don't worry, I'm not going back to school any time soon."

After about an hour of further argument, Jess was gone, and Megan had left, too, crying. David sat down in a chair and, feeling completely exhausted, started thinking. He tried to occupy his mind with random thoughts, but more unhappy thoughts kept butting in. He wasn't really sure what he should try to figure out first. He had lost control with Justin, and less than forty-eight hours later, both his dog and Justin's friend had been murdered. Would Justin really go down for killing a dog just to frame David for killing Sean? David didn't think the idea too farfetched.

He became increasingly angry with himself for putting so much thought into this. There was nothing he could do about anything that was happening, and he didn't feel like talking to anyone about it anymore. He sat in miserable silence; a sick, tormented knot in his stomach convinced him things would only get worse.

After a few moments, he heard a car stop and someone get out and approach his house. He looked out of the tent and saw two men about to knock on the door. He realized that he had known deep down that it would inevitably come to this, and he rolled his eyes at the predictability of it all.

"Hey!" he yelled irritably. "My parents are probably asleep, can I help you?"

The tall man, who was wearing a brown suit, turned around and spoke: "Are you David Slate?"

"Yes," he said, mildly annoyed but not quite losing his composure.

"Do you know a young man by the name of Sean Doyle?"

"Yes. I go to school with him," he replied plainly, showing no emotion and struggling to give off an air of still being unsure why they were interrogating him.

"This, I know," the man sighed. David became less confident upon hearing the man's tone. He seemed as though he were bored with teenage defiance and expected nothing more. Just another day at the office. "I am led to believe that your group of friends and Sean's group of friends do not exactly get along well at school." He remained monotone and sickeningly professional—still bored. "Is this correct?" He looked up from his pocket notebook, apparently already knowing the answer.

"I guess so. They're pretty mean to me and my friends. Mean to everyone, really." David lost any interest in trying to establish his own perspective. He decided not to bother trying to explain that one could scarcely claim that his time at school was spent with a "group of friends."

"Right. Well, as you probably have heard, he was recently murdered, Mr. Slate," he continued in the same, dry tone. The other man, who was shorter and had greasy black hair in a ponytail, never spoke.

"I've heard," David said bluntly.

He smiled sarcastically in a transparent display of proper police-interrogation etiquette. "Well, I am Detective Richardson, and this is Mr. Carl, my partner." He pointed to the short, wide man, who wore a harsh expression and stood with his arms crossed. "We need to wake up your parents and get permission to bring you with us to the station so we can ask you some questions."

"I don't know anything about it. I was here all night sleeping, and I only just read it in the paper a few hours ago." David began feeling defensive again, as well as desperate not to get his parents involved. "It's not like we know that much about each other from school. We're not very close."

"Well, we still need to ask you a few questions, so you'll come with us, Mr. Slate. Either we tell your parents and you get into the car freely, or we tell your parents and you get into the backseat in handcuffs. Which do you choose?"

David sighed, disgusted at the condescending attitude. "Okay, I'll just go inside and tell my mother."

"We'll need to come in with you and talk with them, David," the shorter man interjected with narrowed eyes, almost as if he were afraid that David had some trick up his sleeve and that Detective Richardson would foolishly allow him to go inside alone and do something drastic.

"Why? What's the big deal? I don't want my mom to get the wrong idea and throw a fit." He was becoming increasingly desperate. "Just let me tell her that someone needs to ask me questions about a schoolmate who had an accident and that I'll be home shortly."

"I'm afraid that's out of the question." Mr. Carl seemed to be fighting against an outburst. "Several of your classmates claim that you may be the murderer."

"Classmates?" David yelled, outraged. "No one *witnessed* anything.

They are idiots, and they think that since Justin and I got into a fight the other day that I killed Sean!" David assumed that it was solely Sean's friends to whom Mr. Carl was referring.

Mr. Richardson stepped toward David, seemed to think better of grabbing him, pulled a pen from his pocket, and wrote furiously in his notebook.

"David," Detective Richardson paused and closed his eyes, "You have the right to an attorney, and one will be provided for you if your parents cannot do so. Sean was attacked in the night, but appears to have woken and tried to put up a fight. There were traces of DNA found on and around wounds on his stomach. We need you to answer some questions so that we can narrow down the list of suspects in order to run some tests."

"Yeah, but check the wounds again. Justin and his friends and I got into a fight a few days ago. If my DNA is there, it's days old!"

"So you are admitting that we will find your DNA on Sean?" he asked, leading, sounding interested.

"No! I said that if any of it is mine, it's because of our fight a few days ago!"

Detective Richardson seemed to be getting irritated also. He whispered something to Mr. Carl and turned back to David. "All right, David," he said, "We'll run a few more tests and come back to see you. I'd hate to have to wake your parents or inconvenience you in any way." He seemed eager to relay the possibility of David's DNA being found on Sean's body, probably to turn David's remark into a quasi-confession, but he was pretending to be folding under David's persistence.

"Thank you," David said, grateful nonetheless. "Check for fingerprints. You'll see that there will be none there at Sean's that belong to me. I'll be more than happy to let you test me if you can't figure anything else out."

"Not having fingerprints in the general area is not a strong alibi when compared to not having DNA in open wounds on Sean's stomach," he returned harshly.

"Right, but that happened a few days ago. Just check and you'll see. I know you can put a date on that stuff. How was he killed anyway?"

"He was beaten to death with a metal garbage can lid, which was left in the room." He raised his eyebrow suspiciously. "But no fingerprints were found on it."

David's heart dropped violently, almost making him gag. He should have known. He felt so dumb for not being able to figure it out sooner. "Oh," was all that he could manage.

The detectives seemed to notice his new terror, but they did not persist; they obviously had all they had come for. "Well, thank you for your time. I'm sure we'll be seeing you later." The two detectives walked to the end of the sidewalk and stepped into their car.

36

David sat numbly on the edge of his bed for several minutes, wishing for the comfort of Shaggy. Rather than slowing and calming, his racing heart seemed to be increasing in speed and pounding ever more painfully at his sternum. He could feel with disgusting clarity the tingling in his extremities as each contraction expelled some of his sick, tainted blood. Were the garbage men behind all of it? He hadn't seen the hooded garbage man's face well enough to know whether or not he was old enough to have been involved with Mr. Batterman, but the man's rusty voice made him sound as though he were one hundred and thirty-five years old; the idea was certainly plausible. The bastards had snuck into his tent and killed Shaggy and then immediately turned around and killed Sean, pitting David and Justin against each other even more than they already were, and pretty successfully framing David as well. For the first time, he realized that his house wasn't evil; it was the garbage men who were evil. They were feeding off of his misery and torment, and they just wanted to set up a good finale.

He began to swoon. He steadied himself and decided to bite the bullet and ask Mr. and Mrs. Stewart how in the name of God he would be able to work this out, but he decided that Megan should be his top priority and that he should first hurry to her and make amends. He later wondered briefly whether, if he had simply left the Megan situation as it stood, things would not have come to such a cataclysmic end.

37

David started to Megan's house Desperate with fear and alive with adrenaline, he ran as fast as he could, blood and emotion intensely heating his ears and feeding a fresh headache.

Filled with a confusing sense of urgency, he turned the first corner and began to run faster, each raspy, choked breath violently tearing its way out of his lungs.

By the time David was halfway to Megan's house, the soft tissues in his throat were screaming in agony from the combination of his harsh breaths and the chilly pre-winter air.

When he approached the final turn that would put Megan's house in plain view, David's legs were aching and as quivery as those of a newborn giraffe. His chest was searing, and he began to stumble over each step. His desperation increased, and he felt close to crying due to sheer anxiety.

The sight before David upon rounding the final corner brought him to his hands and knees, wildly heaving for breath. He stared in disbelief at Megan, who was too far away for David to clearly make out her facial expression. She was standing on the sidewalk beside a dark-blue, two-door truck with a God-awful paintjob and huge tires, and directly in front of her with his back against the truck stood Justin Guy.

All concerns of homicidal garbage men and suspicious police and cursed homes with haunted pasts left him. David started to cry silently, kneeling perfectly motionless and never moving his eyes from the scene before him. After he caught his breath, he started to contemplate the situation: why it had happened, how he had let it happen, what he did not yet know, what he would soon find out, and endless other racing thoughts. David felt a nauseating self-pity and cried harder. The aspect that most appalled him was knowing that he was acting out of jealousy. He couldn't allow the possibility that the interaction between Megan and Justin was simply a conversation about the present events; he immediately assumed that their palaver was less than innocent. it wasn't anger toward Justin he felt, not his usual hatred toward him. It was the unfamiliar rage of jealousy. Neither he nor Megan had ever been the least bit jealous; God knew they had no reason to be. He knew that Megan truly loved him and that she would never do anything with anyone to jeopardize the bliss that they shared, and he felt the same way. He would never meet another person who was as genuinely great to him as Megan, and he knew that he would never give her up for petty playfulness with another girl.

But now he felt a sick jealousy writhing in the pit of his stomach like a dying leech struggling to grasp its host. He remained unmoving, increasingly infuriated as he imagined the two of them touching and embracing. He became convinced that he was correct in assuming that their meeting was suspicious once he vividly imagined them kissing—kissing the way that he and Megan had, the way that David himself had, through trial and error, taught her to kiss, the way that they both had developed together over time.

Kissing! Could there possibly exist a more revolting scene? Megan, David's only true love and one of his first true friends, kissing Justin Guy, a nauseating, hillbilly freak? Clones and drones abundantly exist, ever-coating the bottoms of shoes and the undersides of tables! He was scum! He was vile, rancid, pizza-faced scum! He was anything but one-of-a-kind! What could Megan possibly see in him? She certainly couldn't find any quality in Justin Guy that would be scarce in any debauched hallway in any decadent educational institution in this country!

David's tears turned into tiny microcosms of rage, blurring his vision and fueling his fiery hatred, which now extended far beyond Justin Guy and his cohorts. Megan, whom he had given every ounce of trust and compassion, whom he had given everything, had all along been a sneaky traitor, always subtly defending Justin and playing the part of a companion on either side of a petty, nonsensical war that raged on in their pathetic high schools. Megan, whom he had considered the only person in his world, was no different from any other impulsive child—lying, acting, saying, but never thinking. Megan, upon whom he had based his every action, had moved on from him in his time of desperate need with hardly a glance. The more he mused, the more he felt as though he could lift Justin's oversized truck and impale him and Megan right there on the sidewalk. But he sat, unmoving, every organ—every tissue—in his body seeming to contract, struggling to secrete into him a cocktail of every hormone and neurotransmitter. He hardly noticed as his breathing slowed and almost ceased and his jaw slightly slackened. His eyelids relaxed and began to twitch and his ears burned with intense, unnatural pain.

As though a circuit had shorted inside his brain, David remained on his hands and knees for what seemed full minutes, no longer caring about Megan or Justin or garbage men or anything. Nothing of the situation was registering in his mind any longer, and he stared blankly while his best friend and worst enemy said their apparently affectionate goodbyes and parted.

Justin smugly and lazily meandered to his vehicle door and climbed inside. He started the truck and drove directly past David, casting a cursory glance at David splayed awkwardly in the grass, before turning his undivided attention back to his cigarette.

38

"How could you do this to me?" David demanded sharply, at the top of his lungs. He stood and charged forward toward Megan, who had almost made it back to her front porch. "After all we've been through! After everything we've said and done for each other! One day has passed, and you've moved on to a filthy, fucking swine like Justin Guy!"

Megan's eyes widened in surprise at his abrupt appearance and outburst, and, as her shock subsided, she seemed offended. "Are you kidding me?" she asked incredulously.

"I could fucking kill someone right now. I never would have thought that you, of all people, would disappoint me this way."

"David, watch your mouth when you talk to me! You have no idea what you're getting into, and I am not about to stand here and listen to more of your paranoid delusions."

"Paranoid delusions?" he screamed, now almost face-to-face with Megan. "You two were practically holding hands right here while he smoked his cigarette, and it's been, what? A day since you and I had our disagreements?"

"Don't you dare accuse me of holding hands with him, David. I loved you, and if you really think that I would be with someone like Justin—and only a day later, like you said—then I have to wonder how we both fell victim to so many false pretenses." She said this without emotion, as though it were a fact that she had accepted long ago.

"I'm the one who should be worried about false pretenses!" He still was frantic and screaming at the top of his lungs. Nothing she said could console him and make him think or act reasonably again. "You've probably been sneaking around with people like Justin all along. I've just been too naive to notice it!"

"David," she said exasperatedly but not unreasonably, "What

makes you think I'm with Justin? He just stopped to hit on me and give me grief about you, and I told him to get lost. I don't want anything to do with a creep like that. I'm sorry, but you're wrong this time."

"You're lying!" David yelled in her face. "You're a lying, cheating bitch, and I should have known it all along."

Before David finished this sentence, Megan had turned and was wordlessly climbing her steps to go inside. The door slammed and David was engulfed in a seething silence.

After a few moments, he stiffly turned and began walking. His autopilot was taking him back toward his house with no plans, no motives, not even any conscious thoughts.

Vast, thin, gray clouds had overtaken the sky, making the chilly afternoon look hazy. An increasing wind blew as if to clear out any stray objects from the path of a storm. David walked in oblivious silence past the deserted streets and yards, and the only sounds—unheard by him— were the various things blowing in the wind.

He turned a corner, walking around the outside of a stop sign. He walked over a drainage ditch and past two empty yards. He did not notice the large blue truck parked ahead of him, and he did not notice as Justin Guy stepped out holding a portentous metal rod that looked like something out of a New Jersey alleyway.

Justin stood watching David walk, dumbly staring at the ground a few feet in front of him. He cocked his arm behind his head with the pole held high and waited as David expressionlessly approached.

David finally stopped less than five feet from Justin Guy, who stood expectant and poised to strike. As though a switch inside of him was suddenly flicked, David jerkily glanced up to Justin's face, cocked his head, and asked, "Are you fucking kidding me?" just as Justin swiftly brought the rod down across David's temple,

The blow immediately slammed David's head to the right, and the force of it plowed his entire body to the ground. But with a bizarre, jelly-like movement, he seemed to bounce off the concrete like rubber and land back on his feet looking almost amused. Blood rushed from the gash on his head, and his skull looked very likely to be fractured. His senses had come back to him with the blow from the pipe, and he was again filled with unyielding rage toward both Justin and Megan, but his mind was disconnected, and it merely watched without opposition, as though through a red-tinted window, as David took his frustration out on Justin.

He leapt nimbly aside as Justin, who had stumbled in awe, took another swing. Justin lashed out a frustrated backhand, which David easily avoided as he hopped effortlessly backwards and climbed onto the hood of Justin's truck. Justin was big and strong, but that made him too bulky and slow to fight properly.

"You killed my best friend!" Justin sneered.

"Are you kidding me?" David asked again. He had few words to express his revulsion.

Justin swung stupidly and screamed in rage as David stepped aside and watched smugly as the rod crushed the thin metal of the truck's hood.

"My truck!"

He threw the steel rod at David's head, but David easily caught the windmilling pipe with his right hand and spun around to the right to absorb the force. In order to piss Justin off even more, David stared him in the eyes and, with a grin, stabbed the pipe downward into the windshield of the truck. Justin leapt forward and awkwardly failed to climb atop the dented hood. "You're dead, cocksucker!" he called and hustled around the side to open the door.

"Honestly," David said, loftily standing his ground, "That doesn't seem likely right now."

When Justin reached behind his seat and pulled out a small, black pistol and was flicking off the pistol's safety switch. David snorted in mild annoyance and jumped from the truck, landing with one foot planted on each of Justin's shoulders. He bent his knees slightly to absorb the shock of the landing and lashed out his legs again, this time much harder. Justin was flung flat to the ground in one motion, his head slamming against the hard dirt and bouncing back so hard that his chin touched his chest. His arms flailed apart, and David landed, spun, and quickly stomped on the wrist of the hand that was holding the gun. "You're pathetic and slow," he muttered, pulling the gun easily from Justin's dazed fingers and tossing it in the passenger seat of the truck.

Keeping one foot firmly on Justin's wrist, David placed his other foot on his face and watched him writhe as he shifted his weight to it.

"I'll fucking kill you," Justin moaned miserably, his head turned to the side.

"We'll see about that." David bent and lifted Justin by the neck of his shirt and pushed him sideways into the driver's seat of the truck.

"Should I wait for you to come to so it will be a fair fight?" he asked snidely.

"No," Justin groaned. "Give me the gun now."

"Guns, guns, guns," David preached. He suddenly felt more like his usual uneasy self, and he looked away to the right, then to the left, observing the empty streets for no apparent reason. When he looked back at Justin, he had the pistol pointed slightly above David's left shoulder.

David squinted in shock and winced, reaching swiftly forward with both hands and twisting Justin's head by the neck and the chin as the gunpowder simultaneously exploded inches from his ear.

He watched, amazed, as Justin's body suddenly went limp and his torso rolled forward between his legs. He unceremoniously pulled the cadaver out of the truck and onto the ground. How had he snapped his neck so easily?

David backed up, his mouth agape, and placed his arm across his body. His stomach suddenly twisted like a slimy knot of afterbirth, and he barely managed to turn aside before he fell to his knees and dry-heaved on the grass. He couldn't remember the last time he had eaten, and although his reflexes were making his stomach contract, he couldn't produce anything solid. He continued gagging and retching for over a minute.

David looked around frantically, suddenly terrified. He was amazed that Justin had managed to miss his head at such a close range. Even more, he was horrified that he had killed another human, no matter how revolting that person was and despite the fact that it was clearly a case of self-defense. He had already been framed for Sean's murder, and he could think of no alternate reality in which Justin's death could be explained. He figured the garbage men were having themselves a fine old laugh.

He began to cry again as he stood up and ran back toward Megan's house.

39

David no longer thought or cared about a potential relationship between Megan and Justin. He still loved Megan dearly, and she was the only person who could help him now, the only person who could still love him after such an atrocious occurrence. His panicked thoughts did not allow for any future plans or any possible outcomes. He only felt traumatized by what he had done, and he wanted—needed—to have Megan embrace him.

He looked up, still frantically sobbing, and saw Megan far off but hurrying toward him. He began to cry harder and yelled desperately for her.

"He's dead! He's dead! I didn't mean to do it, Megan! I swear! He was trying to kill me, and there was nothing I could do!"

He could see her face now; she was coming toward him but staring determinedly past him, as though she were more worried about Justin at this point. David took no notice; he also didn't notice the green and white garbage truck turn the corner in the distance behind her.

"Justin is dead! He tried to kill me!" he yelled at her again.

Megan stopped running, and David saw the garbage truck quickly approaching. He fell to his knees and began to gasp, forcing air through his choked throat. Tears were streaming down his face. He couldn't speak; he could only manage to point at the truck, still yards behind her, but she didn't seem to notice him at all. She slowly turned of her own accord and looked toward the truck, and then she just stopped and stared, looking horrifyingly scared and confused. "What's going on, David?" she asked, facing the rapidly encroaching garbage truck. He would never forget the way her voice sounded so innocent and oblivious.

As the truck came to a driveway, it swerved to the right so that the two right wheels came over the curb and rolled across the sidewalk, swiftly approaching a still and silent Megan.

"Oh, God! Please, no!" David yelled piercingly and leapt to his feet. He began running toward Megan, but when the truck was just behind her, he was still several yards away.

Just before the truck struck her dead-on, she calmly turned back, staring hopelessly and silently at the ground, and David saw a knowing look of horror come into her eyes. After all of the emotions that her beautiful, bright eyes had conveyed, the last that David ever saw was one that seemed to say, "Please, David. Don't let it end this way. Please."

David did not first think that he and Jess would never be the same or that he would never find out the truth about Megan's infidelities—those thoughts would come later, but only fleetingly—but simply that, in addition to all of the terrible events that had already happened just that day, he was witnessing someone very dear to him brutally murdered, and his mind could not accept it.

He stood with his mouth agape and face glistening as the speeding truck collided with her frail body and sent it hurtling forward. She went limp, and he noticed all-too-clearly the precise moment at which her tired eyes left his and closed forever. She rocketed past him and slammed clumsily into the curb, then slid across the concrete, peeling away parts of her clothing and skin, David knew with sickening certainty that her breastbone and ribs were crushed immediately upon impact. He vaguely noticed as the garbage truck sped past him, swerved back into the road, and turned the corner toward David's own home. One of the garbage men was standing at his post on the back of the truck, and, when they passed, he looked back at David and smiled maliciously. God had given David everything beautiful that he had never known in the form of one single girl, and a grinning, sadistic garbage man had taken it away.

David hurled himself upon the unmoving body of the only person he'd ever loved, and screamed as loudly as he could, wondering how in the hell no one was around in this neighborhood to assist him. He brushed his dirty hand across her perfect face one last time. One of her eyes was slightly open, and it had lost all of its glorious beauty, but her face was still as perfect as it ever was. It looked almost as though she had never been slammed by a speeding, oversized garbage truck.

David sobbed and pleaded with her body not to be dead, not to be gone forever. She had never done a single thing to any living soul to deserve such a death as this. With a wave of paralyzing self-pity, David recalled that his last interaction with her, as with Shaggy, had been far less than favorable. Tears streamed openly down his face and into his mouth as he cursed himself; the thought of his poor, poor Megan dying so abruptly and so violently because of him was nearly enough to make his heart cease to beat.

But one single thought remained that kept his blood flowing, and he scarcely took enough time to stand around and grieve for his lost friend, his love who had once been able to bring him such happiness. He was partially aware and grateful that his rational thoughts had again been clouded by that familiar, vengeful red haze, and he set off toward the garbage men, his face still wet from one of the last innocent and adolescent emotions that he would experience in his life.

40

After sprinting more than halfway home, David realized that the garbage men had almost certainly been going straight to his house, and his sense of urgency increased tenfold. He began to run desperately.

When he finally turned the last corner and his house came into view, David saw that the garbage truck was sitting at the end of his driveway along the curb. He continued to run frantically, becoming less determined and more afraid with every step. He saw that his tent had been destroyed. The canvas was disheveled and collapsed, draped over all of his belongings. He could see the outline of his dresser, desk, and bed underneath. As he came closer and noticed that his front door was standing open, his fear mounted, and, with a sense of portentous finality, he wondered if he should go inside at all.

He sped along his driveway, leapt up the steps in front of the door, and stepped through the doorway. His eyes were wide, and his heart was racing. All of the lights in the house were off, and, in the dim late afternoon, everything looked gloomy. He started to call for his mother, but he could manage to do little more than squeak. Even that minute sound was hushed when one of the garbage men stepped around the corner with his finger against his lips in a shushing gesture. His hood was up, as usual, and in the faint light of the kitchen his face was completely in shadow. David again noticed the caustic glow of his eyes. His knees buckled and became shaky, and his insides quivered. Once again he had lost all of his composure when confronted with one of the garbage men. The red haze was gone, and he felt nothing but an extreme sense of helplessness. Even if he had thought about it, he likely could not have even run across the street to get help from Mr. Stewart.

David felt exhausted and overwhelmed, and he wanted desperately to lie down and cry himself to sleep. "Please," he begged, "I can't take this anymore."

"Yes. It does seem like things have been blown outrageously out of proportion, don't it?" the man replied nonchalantly in his dry, rasping voice. The sound of it sent chills of dread down David's spine.

"What do you want?" he asked, crying again.

"Ain't it obvious?" the garbage man replied simply. "What do you want, David?"

"I want this to end. I want it to stop. I want you to take back the things that you've done—but I know that you can't do that."

"Is that really what ya want? What use is there in wanting things you never can get?"

David felt anger beginning to invade his grief. "Yes!" he screamed. "I'm not playing these stupid games with you!"

The garbage man smiled at David's childish outburst. His silver teeth shone dully. "I thought it would be this way." He nodded slightly and David felt two unbearably strong hands come down on his shoulders. He did not need to look around to know who was there, so he remained still in spite of his sudden fright. His eyes widened pleadingly at the man in front of him, but the garbage man only grinned. "Come," he said while turning aside and walking into the living room.

David began to struggle and tried to pull away, so the garbage man behind him pulled David's arms snugly behind his back and locked them in place with his own arms. David felt his feet lifted effortlessly off the ground as he was carried through the kitchen and into the living room. He heard the door slam shut behind them.

41

When they entered David's living room, he saw that his parents were kneeling on the floor side-by-side, both bound and gagged with towels and rags from around the house. He looked at them with a sick pity and saw that they were both looking at him—not at the garbage men, but at him—wearing matching expressions of revulsion, the familiar matching expressions that they wore any other day of the year.

The garbage man hurled David's limp body into a chair in the corner, where he sat unmoving and let out a small, choked sob. He no longer felt physically able to move or speak. The garbage man who had been restraining him obviously knew this, for he made no further effort to hold David back. The other garbage man stepped behind his parents, who were still scowling silently at David alone as if they knew what was going to happen and wanted him to know that, no matter what, they would hate him forever and after.

When the man in his outrageous black jumpsuit bent over and picked up a small, sharp kitchen knife, David hung his head and closed his eyes. The other man immediately walked behind the chair and grasped each side of David's head and forced it upright, making him cry out in pain for the first time from the wound inflicted earlier by Justin's pipe. His hair was matted with dried blood, and his head was severely swollen and bruised.

The garbage man behind Pete and Janet Slate placed the knife momentarily inside the pocket on the front of his jumpsuit and placed one hand on each of David's parents' heads. Before David had time to register what he was doing, the man brutally smashed their heads together in one swift movement. David jumped at the suddenness of the action; the sound of his parents' skulls simultaneously crushing echoed through the otherwise silent room. They both fell forward and lay in a heap on the floor.

David's sobs became more pronounced and frequent, and tears were streaming down his face. He was forced to watch uselessly as the man pulled the knife back from his pocket, bent over his father, and pushed the blade into the side of his neck. The only sounds that David could hear were his own choking sobs, the rustle of the garbage man's sleeves, and a sickening sound like a small water balloon popping. David cried harder as he watched thick, hot blood pour out of the wound. The garbage man grasped Pete's hair and slid the knife through the skin all the way across his throat. David's father never moved nor made a sound through the whole process. David couldn't even tell when he took his last breath.

Blood collected rapidly and formed a sick pool on the blue rug where Pete was lying. When the garbage man finally pulled the knife out of his father's throat, he startled David again by lunging forward and beating the knife into Pete's gut. He stood up and grasped the knife handle in both hands and bent over Pete again, repeatedly lunging the blade into his soft, fat belly.

The man continued mutilating the corpse until Pete's shirt was in tatters and his stomach seemed to be nothing more than a hole, a gore-filled crater in which the garbage man continued to pound both fists. Blood and adipose and portions of other tissues flew wildly in the air each time the garbage man drew back his fists. David was too appalled to even scream.

Finally the man stood upright, his chest heaving wildly. He never looked up toward David. He turned and bent again, this time holding a hot clothing iron that he must have plugged in especially for the occasion. Without missing a beat, the man stooped and kneeled beside his mother, who was now moving slightly. David glanced over at his mother's eyes and saw that they were now opened halfway. Her face was covered with blood from the blow that she took earlier and with bits of her husband's insides. She was breathing irregularly and struggling to move away, obviously still in pain and not fully conscious. By now David could sense a pleading look in her half-lidded eyes, but there was nothing that he could do. Even the knowledge that he would be next could not incite him to act.

The garbage man rolled his mother from her side to her stomach and pulled up her shirt, revealing her back. She was biting hard on the cloth in her mouth, and David could see tears streaming down her face as well. When the garbage man pushed the hot iron down on the small of her back, she cried out faintly and weakly. David heard with grotesque detail her skin sizzle and tighten beneath the heat of the iron. The garbage man even went out of his way to mockingly press the button to spray water onto her burning back. David could sense that the garbage man who was still holding his throbbing head was smiling sadistically. Janet continued to groan hoarsely while the man straddling her sprayed her skin to moisten it and slowly pulled the iron across her lower back. David continued to cry increasingly intensely as he watched her body jerk convulsively with every choked sob.

These were his parents, no matter how terrible they may have been. Regardless of their cruelties, David would never have wished something this horrific on either of them, or on anyone, for that matter. He cried harder and harder, sitting helplessly in the chair. He yearned faintly for Megan, but his thoughts of her were muddled by his distress.

The garbage man on top of his mother's now-unconscious body reached down to the ground, retrieved the bloody knife, and cut Janet's shirt completely apart to expose her upper back. David started to get angry. His helplessness made him feel claustrophobic, and he shook violently, with tears still pouring into his slightly open mouth.

When the man behind him noticed David's shaking, he moved his strong hands from David's head back to his shoulders to hold him steady, but he still did not say a word. The other garbage man threw the iron away, stood, and stretched lazily. He paused for a moment and then began to look around the room, as if something were missing. He finally walked over to a coffee table, picked it up, and held it at a measured angle above Janet's head. When David realized what was going to happen, he cried out. The garbage man brought the edge of the table down into the nape of Janet's neck. David saw her neck crush beneath the weight of the table and her head loll unnaturally as though the bones inside had come apart completely.

Finally the garbage man tossed the table aside and faced David. He approached the chair and glared at David sternly, as if the previous affair had to be done because of him. David's heart pounded wildly at the thought of what the monster had in store for him now: the grand finale. But after a few moments, the man glanced up at his partner and tilted his head toward the door, clearly indicating that they should go.

42

David sat in still silence for a few minutes, astounded but not in the least bit comforted that the garbage men had spared his life. His eyes remained wide, wet, and shocked, and he leaned forward between his legs and retched. His head ached savagely when his entire body contracted and convulsed, but after a few minutes, he finally stopped gagging and was able to stand up on unsteady legs.

Eager to vacate the gory, blood-splattered living room, he ran frantically into the kitchen, his mind almost irreversibly destroyed by now. When he looked out the window, he saw one of the garbage men walking up the driveway of the Stewarts' house, and he struggled to regain his senses.

"No. No! No!" he muttered, suddenly motivated to end this once and for all. He turned back to glance one final time at the mangled corpses of his parents. Despite all the cruelty and wickedness they had displayed, the sight nauseated David completely, and he inexplicably longed for a time when things were at the very least simpler. Subconsciously he knew that his entire world had changed in the blink of an eye, and nothing would ever again lend him a sense of normalcy.

No good would ever come of this house. There was no question in David's mind that his only option was to destroy it. He quickly walked to the old-fashioned stove, turned the gas as high as it would go, and clicked on the pilot. A large and infirm flame flared up in front of his face and flickered unstably. He grabbed a roll of paper towels and threw it across the room, and then he balled up a mass on the other end of the roll and threw it into the flame. The tissue immediately combusted, and the thin paper along the roll burned feebly. Desperate, David opened various cabinets and pulled out every cleaning product that he could find. He opened them all quickly and began pouring them around the kitchen. He threw glass bottles of alcohol against the wall and into the flames.

Finally, he ran into the garage and found a can of gasoline, which he took back into the house and poured all over the walls, floors, counters, and onto his parents' bodies. He placed the half-empty can between their disfigured corpses.

Before leaving, he picked up what was left of the roll of paper towels, made sure that it was lit, and threw it into a puddle of gasoline, which exploded into a flame that engulfed his entire field of vision.

Not bothering to close the door behind him, David ran outside and started across the street, but he stopped halfway and turned to look one last time at the house that had caused all of his woes. He saw the foggy scar on the top left corner of the tiny attic window vanish as black smoke clouded every ounce of air inside. He saw the out-of-place fresh layer of paint over the railing of the small front porch sizzle and melt off of the burning wood. He saw the round stained-glass window above the garage door shatter with the sudden explosion from the gas can. He watched the carved birdlike shapes at the top of the porch posts blaze brilliantly in front of the hellish flames that would doubtlessly put an end to this forsaken house.

He finally ran across the street and into the open front door of the Stewarts' house. "Hey!" he called desperately. His voice squeaked because he was so hoarse. "Mr. Stewart! Look out! Quick!" He was vaguely aware that Mrs. Stewart's car was gone, so he found a little comfort in assuming she was not at home.

He ran through their dark house, searching every room for a sign of Mr. Stewart or the garbage men, and he continued to call out for them, filled with dread.

In Mr. Stewart's bedroom, David noticed that the closet door was open, and saw a trunk and a heap of clothes strewn on the floor. He cautiously approached the pile, paralyzed with fear at what he might find on the other side. When he was close enough, he saw a hidden trapdoor in the floor, which was also standing open. Frantic to save Mr. Stewart and thinking nothing of how weird it was to have a trapdoor in a closet, he jumped over the rubble and began descending the stairs underground without a second thought.

When he reached the bottom of the stairs, the trapdoor above him slammed shut with a crash, and all light was lost.

"Mr. Stewart! Mr. Stewart! Mr. Stewart! Mr. Stewart! Mr. Stewart!" he begged wildly, clinging blindly to the wall.

In the distance he heard shuffling and murmuring. He plopped down upon the ground and clutched the wall frenetically, again crying and calling out Mr. Stewart's name in a high-pitched voice.

He heard the shuffling approaching and noticed that the murmuring had stopped. "Oh, God! Please help! Please stop this! Mr. Stewart!" David continued to bawl hysterically, too afraid to attempt to climb back up the stairs, until he felt certain that he could reach out and touch the source of the shuffling. He pressed his body against the wall helplessly and held his breath until he heard the click as someone's dry lips parted.

Suddenly a hand grasped his throbbing forehead and smashed the back of his head into the wall, rendering him unconscious.

43

David awoke some time later bound with rope to an uncomfortable old wooden chair. His head ached horrendously, and his neck screamed in protest when he lifted his head after such an extended period of inactivity.

He was in a vast room that appeared to be decked-out like a garage. The walls, floor, and ceiling were all hard, packed dirt, but all around the room were shelves and racks filled with old, dusty, and rusty garden tools, containers, buckets, cords, ropes, and spare parts to various machines. The only lights were two medieval-looking torches mounted on the walls on either side of the room, and David could see numerous dark, narrow hallways branching out from this seemingly central dome.

He looked around feeling terrified and confused. He was too afraid to call out for help. Suddenly he heard mumbling from behind him, and he turned to see Mr. Stewart walking aimlessly along the wall, seeming deep in thought.

"Mr. Stewart!" David called instinctively.

Mr. Stewart started and looked over at David. "Oh, David! You're awake. Forgive me. I can't remember where I put my . . ." his voice trailed off musingly, increasing David's confusion.

"I don't—" David began, suddenly feeling a knot in his stomach more foreboding than any before.

"No matter," Mr. Stewart said. He suddenly looked at David with businesslike disgust. "I shall make do without it. How do you feel, David?"

"I feel— " He paused, confused.

"Murderous?" Mr. Stewart asked with a smile.

"What is this?" David demanded. His eyes were widening incredulously. "This can't be—"

"I beg your pardon?" Mr. Stewart pretended to misunderstand.

"You're with them?" David's voice was pleading for Mr. Stewart to deny his notions.

"With whom?" Mr. Stewart smiled viciously.

David swore that he wouldn't cry helplessly again, but Mr. Stewart's games were making him feel antsy. He sat in an intense silence.

"You mean the—who was it for you again? The garbage men?"

"What are you talking about? This is crazy. Let me go!"

Mr. Stewart sighed with sarcastic sincerity. "David, do you really believe this?"

"No. To be honest with you, I can't believe any of this! I looked up to you. You were like a father to me. And now what is this? Is Mrs. Stewart in on it too?"

"Mrs. Stewart is what she is."

"What's that supposed to mean?" David demanded.

"It means that Mrs. Stewart doesn't need to know about anything that will upset her! Got it?" He lunged at David and slapped his face, sending searing pain into David's wounded head.

"Yeah! Yeah!" David started becoming angry again; he struggled and writhed against his bindings, but they didn't give at all. He had risked his life to come into Mr. Stewart's house to protect him. "I trusted you. I looked up to you. And you had me duped from day one . . ."

Mr. Stewart rolled his eyes. "Okay, out with your sob story."

"No. I'm serious. You were a real friend to me. I always respected you a lot." David now wore a scowl, and he could feel the red haze settling in. "You had me and my friends scared and believing in some stupid curse. And now my friends are dead!" He remembered Megan's battered body; he remembered the last thing that he had said to her and fought hard against making himself even more vulnerable by crying yet again.

"Jess is still alive, if I'm not mistaken," Mr. Stewart cut in quickly. "Would you like to have him killed too?"

"You leave him alone!" David yelled.

"It isn't I. Those killings are your doings, David. I'll let you go now, and I feel pretty certain that Jess will die."

David, for one merciful second, believed that Mr. Stewart knew nothing of the garbage men and had David tied solely because he thought that David was the one on a killing spree. "I haven't done any of this! It's the garbage men! You have the wrong idea!"

Mr. Stewart laughed humorlessly. "So naive. There are no garbage men, David, at least not the ones that you believe you've seen."

"It was you!" he bawled, his hope crashing down around him.

Mr. Stewart shook his head. "The garbage men do not exist. They are a figment of your imagination."

"No! I dreamt of them, and then they were here! They predicted everything that would happen! They killed my friends! My family! They were real!" David could now longer fight it, and he was crying tears of frustration.

"David!" Mr. Stewart yelled. "Enough! The human mind is a powerful weapon. I happen to know how to manipulate the minds of others quite well, and the sooner you realize that you were manipulated, the sooner we may proceed!"

David sat unbelievingly. Mr. Stewart was a completely different person. Even his voice was different. His kindly southern drawl had completely vanished.

"I planted the idea of the curse in your head. I planted the idea of Mr. Batterman in your head. That is all that it took for your imagination to run wild. I just sat back and enjoyed the show."

"No," David could think of nothing more to say.

"I'm afraid so, David."

"You're wrong. The curse is real. The garbage men are real." He didn't know what to believe anymore.

"What a silly thing to say," Mr. Stewart said through a mocking smirk.

"I felt different in that house!" David yelled defiantly.

"Aren't you listening? I planted that idea. Your mind did all the rest! You felt different because you wanted to feel different. You thought you should."

"What about my dreams?" David pleaded. He was certain that Mr. Stewart couldn't be telling the truth.

"You met someone. You had déjà vu. Your mind substituted familiar faces for unfamiliar ones from a dream. It's a common phenomenon."

"What—" David struggled to think of a way to go on. "Then who killed them? Who killed my family?" He was weeping openly now.

Mr. Stewart's quiet stare was enough of an answer.

"No," David stated simply.

"Yes."

"No." He thought of the way that Shaggy cowered away from him the night before he died, and he began to sob helplessly. "I loved Megan," he cried, "I would have done anything for her."

"Yes, David, you would do just about anything for just about anything. You're pathetic. It's what made you such an easy target. You've lived your whole life trying to please other people. You have to learn to find what you want and take it!"

"No," David said again. He so desperately wanted for this to be a lie.

"You dreamt a premonition of who would die, correct? You were destined to kill them yourself. You said that the garbage man predicted the future," he paused to let this sink in for David, "But only you can predict your future, David. It was just a character in your mind stating the things that you, deep down, aimed to do." He added slowly and deliberately, "Self fulfilling prophecy."

"Why would I want to kill them?" He thought of the look of pleading terror in Megan's eyes before she died, the way she seemed unable to see him as he warned her about the truck he would have sworn had actually been there, the way his mind was increasingly frequently disconnecting from his body.

"Well, not necessarily that you wanted to," Mr. Stewart continued bitterly, "Just that you would. I knew that you would. You have a lot of pent-up emotion."

"But," David thought wildly for any loophole, any way to disprove this madness, "What about . . . about Mr. Batterman?" He paused. "What about all the others?"

"Mr. Batterman may or may not have existed. As for the others, they fell into my trap just as easily as you, but you were an interesting subject."

"So this is some kind of game to you?"

He thought of the way that his parents scowled at him, never regarding the two garbage men walking around them.

"Hmm, I suppose you could say that." Mr. Stewart smiled sadistically. "We're in the final round. This one is non-scoring." He tilted his head toward one of the corridors. "The others are all down there."

David imagined a small heap of rotted dead bodies that this twisted old man had collected over the years, a mound of pawns in his mind-trip revolution.

"Don't you know the police will find you? You can't keep killing people who move into the house across the street and get away with it forever."

"What evidence links me to those people?" Mr. Stewart demanded harshly. " If he's interrogated, will Jess point me out as a suspect? Would you have suspected that I was behind a number of murders?"

Of course, David would never have suspected such a dear friend.

Mr. Stewart continued, "This isn't a Hollywood drama, David. There are no super-cop investigators in Thriftson County who will discover obscure clues and start looking in this direction! The truth is, no one knows what goes on with all these families. People are coming and going from houses on this block every month. In the real world, David, unsolved crimes simply lose appeal and disappear."

David thought of the way Megan kept her back turned to him moments before she died, the way she stared unblinkingly at the truck. He thought vaguely that he could see himself sitting behind the wheel of that imaginary truck, a nonexistent conveyer of blunt, violent trauma. He thought of the dangers of the human mind.

As though reading his thoughts, Mr. Stewart stated, "The human mind is a beautiful thing. Unfortunately, many people, like you, possess weak ones."

"I'm not weak." He thought of the way that his mother's eyes seemed to plead for him to stop while she was dying, while he was killing her.

"You're feeble-minded."

"I'm not." His red curtain continued to descend. He hated himself for allowing himself to become another part of this old man's stupid game. He hated Mr. Stewart for what he said he'd done. He hated every moment ever leading up to this sick, demented torment. He could not have killed Megan. He could not have killed Shaggy and his parents.

"It's hardly worth arguing over. I have made up my mind. I know how to manipulate minds. I will continue to do this until my time is up. I will continue to ponder the fabric of the psyche."

David smiled at this, feeling confident and rebellious behind the shade of his haze. "No you won't." He thought of the way Megan's corpse had looked like it was never impaled by a speeding truck. He thought of all the lives that Mr. Stewart had ruined with his psychotic manipulation.

"Oh?" Mr. Stewart feigned interest.

"Nope. That house is burning as we speak."

"You forget, Mr. Slate, the house was never cursed. There are no curses, there are no premonitions, there is no divinity, there were never any homicidal garbage men, and there is no magic. There are only the wonders of the mind." He spread his hands in front of David's bleeding head. "There will be more houses, more curses to construct."

"Your obsession is a little creepy." David withheld his composure. "Then I'll have to stop you myself."

Mr. Stewart threw his head back and laughed heartily as if he found this quite amusing. David's body tightened, and, as he strained, the fibers of the rope weakened imperceptibly.

"Bad things happen to good people, David. This will continue to be true even after I am gone. Spare me your pity party and prospect of the greater good." Mr. Stewart turned toward one of his shelves.

"Bad people do bad things to good people," David retorted relentlessly.

Obviously annoyed, Mr. Stewart turned back slowly. "Great people do great things to weak people." The words came out slowly and deliberately. "There will always be those in opposition to research."

After a heated stare, Mr. Stewart grimaced and turned back toward his tools.

Stalling and suddenly mildly curious, David asked, "What about the pine tree?"

Mr. Stewart pointed toward another dark corridor without turning his head. "Down there. Just a natural phenomenon."

"Just another part of your bogus story."

Mr. Stewart sighed as he bent and picked up a chainsaw. "Well, this is a little melodramatic, but I cannot find my carving kit. As I said, it will have to do."

"Carving kit? A chainsaw?" He no longer feared death. "You're ridiculous." The red curtain had descended upon David for the final time.

44

David could almost taste the adrenaline coursing through his bloodstream. "Tell me," he said as Mr. Stewart came back to face him and closed in to within two feet of him, "Should I tell Mrs. Stewart the truth, or should I spare her the heartache of knowing that her husband was a weak, sleazy coward who gets off on twisted mind-fucks and mutilation?"

Mr. Stewart scowled and swiftly jerked his arm to ignite the chainsaw's motor. It roared to life in a deafening explosion that paralleled David's own explosive movement. He suddenly freed his arms and legs from their fraying shackles, which were futile when compared to the power of his red haze.

He slid downward in the chair and flung both feet upward into the bottom of Mr. Stewart's chin, slamming him hard enough to crack multiple teeth and break the skin. The chair flipped backward, rolling David back and onto his feet, and Mr. Stewart stumbled backwards feebly and dropped the heavy chainsaw, which spun and cut a huge gash in his shin.

David merely smiled. "You may be witty and sharp, but you're just not cut out for the physical stuff anymore, Mr. Stewart."

The room was once again silent, as the chainsaw's engine had died upon hitting the hard ground. David's ears were ringing.

"You'll suffer more than the others," Mr. Stewart spat through the blood in his mouth.

"We've done our share of suffering," David replied while reaching with both hands for the nearest objects, a hammer and a hatchet hanging side-by-side on a rack on the wall. Aware that Mr. Stewart was quickly approaching from behind, David whirled around to the right, swinging the hammer that was turned backwards in his left hand. The sharp, curved claw of the hammer penetrated Mr. Stewart's skull easily and drove him to his knees. His eyes widened for the last time, and a mist of blood sprayed from his open mouth. He kneeled at David's feet, wide-eyed and still breathing but unable to move, completely paralyzed by his sudden brain trauma. In one final movement, David torqued the hammer's curvature upward, making Mr. Stewart lift his face toward his own, and nimbly swung the hatchet at Mr. Stewart's neck; he succeeded in nearly removing his entire head. At the same time, he planted his right foot on Mr. Stewart's chest and kicked. As the body flung backwards onto the ground, the hammer peeled away a large portion of the skull and shoveled out a chunk of brain matter.

David threw down the hammer and hatchet in sudden disgust. He fell to his knees, breathing savagely in the old man's blood. Suddenly the insanity of the day's most recent events caught up with him, and he grew insurmountably fatigued. He felt, if nothing else, grateful that he could now sleep.

Struggling not to collapse, he looked around the silent, under-ground room. With his head beginning to slump and his eyelids droop-ing dangerously, he thought that he could see a tall, black, hooded figure with glowing green eyes walking slowly towards him out of the gloom of one of the corridors.

45

David opened his eyes.

His mind was torn apart by trauma and tranquilizers.

His head was leaning lazily against a window in an unfamiliar vehicle.

He sat alone, restrained.

He could make out indistinct blurs zooming by outside.

David closed his eyes . . .

46

David opened his eyes.

He struggled to lift his weary head, which was still planted against the window.

He fought against nausea and blinked his eyes repeatedly until he could vaguely make out images.

His arms were restrained, but he did not feel claustrophobic. He could not rightly remember if he had ever had a fear of tight spaces.

He could not rightly remember his name at the moment.

He allowed his head to rest against the window again and closed his eyes . . .

47

David opened his eyes.

He was sitting in an uncomfortable wooden chair with his arms restrained.

His head ached horrendously, and his neck screamed in protest when he lifted his head from the window.

He looked around the room, which seemed to be all white. There was a bed against one wall, a steel door with a tiny, reinforced glass window, the chair in which he was sitting, and, beside his head, a window that was reinforced even more strongly.

The window overlooked a lush, green courtyard with two trees devoid of their leaves, a couple benches, flowerbeds, sidewalks, and a pond. In the distance he could see endless trees as though he were surrounded by forest.

There were bright fluorescent lights in the ceiling that illuminated the shiny white tile floors and forced his tired eyes to squint.

He looked back out the window and noticed a bird suddenly take flight as a small child released her mother's hand and ran towards it.

Birds . . . always on their guard, yet completely brainless. How can anything so ignorant have enough sense to get away from something as simple as a human when it needs to?

He grinned at the humorless notion. It seems that everyone is out to get them . . .

Perhaps humans are a lot like birds . . .

Humans . . . always on their guard, yet completely feeble-minded. How can anything so magnificently evolved not have enough sense to get away from something as simple as its own mind? This notion made him grin more widely, but he had no idea why.

In his current state, he had no idea what it even meant.

His head hurt intensely.

David closed his eyes . . .

48

David opened his eyes.

He was standing on his bed, and his arms were finally free.

Vaguely, far-off, he wondered how he had gotten here.

He was standing still with something thick wrapped around his neck. He glanced down and saw that the sheet was off his bed. Could this be—?

Could it work? David smiled at the humorless notion.

Where was the other end of the sheet tied?

Vaguely, far-off, he wondered how he was going to manage to pull off this feat.

He closed his eyes . . .

49

David opened his eyes.

He was losing his balance and falling forward.

Vaguely, far-off, he thought he felt a hand prodding his back, urging him from the edge of the bed.

His feet slid off the mattress, and he fell only a few inches.

His neck did not jar. He felt weightless. His breathing gradually slowed, and his vision gradually blurred.

He forced his eyes open and lazily glanced toward the door while he swung slowly back and forth from the ceiling by his neck.

He indistinctly thought that he could make out a tall, hooded figure in a black jumpsuit turn away from him and walk right through his reinforced steel door.

He smiled at nothing in particular.

Vaguely, far-off, although he knew not why, he felt as though he had succeeded, as though he had done something good and that this was the way things had to be. He knew that he had made mistakes along the way, and he knew that, as a result, things would never be the same. He would die alone, friendless, and shivering, warmed not even by his own blood.

David closed his eyes . . .

50

Jess opened his eyes.

His head was resting against his bedroom window, and he was grieving over his great losses. His best friend had allegedly short-circuited and killed his girlfriend, his enemies, his parents, and his neighbor. Even his own dog. Not to mention, he burned down his house. Now he was wasting away in some facility, constantly drugged, not even able to remember the atrocities of his recent past.

When Jess awoke fully, he felt the sick knot creep back into his stomach, and his eyes began to water anew. God had given him all that a kid could want, had, for about three months, made him feel like Superman. But now his eyes were open to what little good there existed in the world, and he felt worse than ever.

He watched two birds brutally argue and exchange blows in his lawn.

Miserably thinking that birds, with their savagery, were a lot like humans, he closed his eyes . . .